FIRST CENTURY CONVERSATIONS

FIRST CENTURY CONVERSATIONS

By James Comfort Smith

Founded 1910
THE CHRISTOPHER PUBLISHING HOUSE
HANOVER, MASSACHUSETTS 02339

Library of Congress Catalog Number 97-75021

ISBN: 0-8158-0533-0

PRINTED IN THE UNITED STATES OF AMERICA

Dedication

These lines are dedicated to my wife
Kathryn
who has made life a constant
and consistent joy

Table of Contents

The enclosed "conversations" are not to be taken as historical. They are completely the product of creative imagination. While I have endeavored to be true to such limited information as Scripture gives us, none of the material herein beyond Scripture is necessarily historical.

Preface

Those eternally hopeful individuals who, wisely or unwisely, occupy a pulpit, learn early in the game that Sunday comes once every seven days with an almost vicious regularity. The Lord of all, including time, is unimpressed that the preceding week has been a series of twelve-hour days and long committee-nights: the pressing calls to the hospital, the personal cultivation of new members and the personal calming of nervous or resentful older members, the attention due his or her associates on staff, the expected community involvements and all the rest — do not one whit slow the terrible march of the week toward Sunday morning and that demanding pulpit. The pressure is intensified when, as in the present case, the majority of years in that pulpit have been spent in communities that are the habitat of major universities; slipshod thinking or shallow preparation haven't slipped by undetected...

It was an April in which, like most other Aprils, Easter was fast approaching. Sitting in my tower study, safely away from telephones and other enemies, I was struggling with the problem of what one says on Easter that has not been said a thousand times before by far more able crafters of good preaching than oneself. Idly penciling a scratch tablet, I found myself writing a note, a first-person experience, of watching the passing procession to Calvary.

Suddenly, captured by the idea, I thought of Simon of Cyrene who had more than a little part in that procession — and I was on my way. The resulting series of letters to his wife back at home in that Mediterranean south-shore city became my Easter message.

The reaction on the part of the congregation was unexpected. More than one worshipper remarked that never before had he/she genuinely experienced Easter as they had always longed to do — and that now they knew what that meant.

I followed the genre frequently over the years that lay ahead, particularly at Christmas and Easter. As time went by, and the requests came again and again, I began to wonder what might result if I tried to put some of these experiences down on paper, usually in very different form and far more detailed than is proper to the pulpit. The present volume is the result...

I have found myself seeking to speak to the doubter of things Christian, as well as to the devoted. Strict orthodoxy has never interested me: the essential and personal Christian claim always has. I have found myself constantly in the writing process speaking without conscious intention to the struggler — the one who longs for a personal involvement in faith, but who rarely seems to find it. I hope that such ones may find some handles here to which to hold steadfastly.

I would hope, too, that the preacher searching for some new freshness in his thought and presentation, might find inspiration here to embark on new seas.

My thanks are due to so many who have influenced both thought and determination, particularly: to my father, Herbert Booth Smith, one of the great masters of the American pulpit in his day; to Robert McAfee Brown, himself a writer of books that people read, who has been quietly encouraging; to Dr. Kenneth Doane of California State University, Fullerton, who refused to leave me alone in an unwritten state; and particularly to my publishing consultant, Dr. Roland W. Tapp, who has forced my hand with wit, humor and wisdom.

Los Gatos, 1998

BOOK ONE

The Bethlehem Connection

Chapter 1

A Shepherd Speaks

Yes, I was up there on the hill today: Golgotha, they call it. I watched the whole thing. Most of the people who were there are struggling with shock and amazement like mine, amazement at how he took it — how silent he was as they put him on the cross. Occasionally his lips seemed to move in prayer, but that was all. It wasn't a pleasant thing to watch, I can assure you.

There's already a feeling in some quarters that his trial was so shallow as to be brutally unjust...I don't know much about such things; few of us shepherds do. I wouldn't exchange the quiet, free life we live for all of your city ways.

But — that man this morning. He wasn't your ordinary man; I'm convinced of it now. I *should* have been convinced a long time ago — many years ago, in fact. I had my chance; it was all right there in front of me. But I was very young, and more than ordinarily thoughtless, I'm afraid...

At any rate, the truth didn't dawn on me until yesterday.

It was about noon, and he was talking to a group of us near the Pool of Siloam. He mentioned that he had been born in Bethlehem, and afterward I spoke to him. He told me a little about his birth in our town, just down the road here — and suddenly I knew. I had been there: I was present at that birth...

Yesterday I spoke to him; today he's dead — or certainly most people would say he's dead... I — well, we'll be at Bethlehem soon; it's around that far bend along the top of this ridge and on about half a league; it's a bit beyond to where we're grazing the flock. Would you walk with me there? Perhaps I can make you understand why I'm confused about this man, this Nazarene. The field we're on with the flock right now is the field where it all began...

It was well over thirty years ago. I was in my early twenties, the junior of the group of us who worked the fields around Bethlehem with our ceremonial flocks, sheep principally intended for temple use in the Sacrifice. They were uncommonly fine animals.

I was not a religious youth, you must know. The shepherd's lot in life doesn't permit him to be at worship with any regularity. But this was of no concern to me; I was healthy and young, and my tomorrows seemed always a long way off. My days and nights in the open air with congenial company, the far distances, the campfire at night — these things were enough and I thought little about much else.

The other three fellows were good men and good company. There was Marcus, warm and musical, whose songs and lyre made our campfires vibrant with joy or soft with a sort of melancholy. He was only a few years older than I... And Simon: a convinced patriot, Simon. He trusted staunchly that the world had been created by a Hebrew God to be ruled by the Hebrew nation... But Simon was a kindly man, and just.

And then there was Alpheus.

How can I describe Alpheus to you? The years had crowned his head with a thick, venerable snow. His eyes could be uncomfortably piercing, but most of the time Alpheus looked out upon his world with a benign, intelligent gaze that suggested the scholar and the mystic — for he was both... I was convinced that if ever there was a man who walked with God, that man was Alpheus.

He was not often at public worship, I suppose, for he had spent his life as a shepherd and he was devoted to his calling. Much of the time, though, there was a scroll in his hand or tucked under his arm, and in moments of relaxation you could expect to find him reading under a sycamore.

Alpheus was frequently in prayer... Often, when I was unable to sleep during the night hours and it was Alpheus' turn to be on guard, I used to watch him kneeling there beneath the stars. During the day, although he was good company and enjoyed us as we enjoyed him, Alpheus never objected to lone watches; I've seen him return after a two-day hunt for strays alone in the wilderness, and never mention having felt lonely. Alpheus would have told you that he was never alone... In those carefree days, I regarded this as an amiable eccentricity. I have since come to understand what he meant: in truth, Alpheus never was alone. Alpheus loved us as we loved him, but he didn't *need* us as we needed him. Alpheus didn't need anyone: he walked with God.

The days and the weeks and the seasons passed uneventfully and with great contentment. Then, without warning, there came a change.

It all hinged around a child... The details of the thing are so strange and so difficult to accept that I've long since learned to keep them to myself. But — this man they crucified this morning. He's brought it all back. I — I still can't accept what's pressing in on me with such intensity; I find myself both confused and distraught. But — let me tell it to you simply as I remember it, tell it as it's being forced in upon me from yesterday's conversation...

It was a cool night, with the smell of winter in the soft breeze. I remember that we had been in a wakeful mood, and we'd built a bigger fire than usual with the idea of talking awhile as we lay and watched the stars.

Our manner of life was not given to much tension. There were those rare occasions, of course, when a marauding animal was near or when a poacher tried to steal from the flock in the weary post-midnight hours. For the most part, though, our days and nights passed in a peaceful routine.

On this night, though, I remember feeling on edge. It was no more than a slight unease, a minor nervousness, but the others must have felt it too. None of us, as I've said, was in a mood for sleep.

Conversation died down and for a couple of hours there was silence — but still I knew that the others were awake. Breathing was irregular, and frequently one of them would turn in his blanket.

It must have been shortly before midnight that Alpheus arose quietly from his pallet and moved off to where a little rise in the ground gave a commanding view of the country about us. Some little distance away from our usual campfire clearing, it was a favorite point of vantage for us; we could see almost the entire flock at once during grazing hours.

I lay watching Alpheus silently, and I discovered that the others, awake, had watched him too. He reached the small hillock and promptly knelt in prayer... It wasn't unusual for Alpheus to be in prayer; it *was* unusual for him to rise and pray at this time of night.

Alpheus had been there, head bowed, for five minutes or so when my attention was caught by the sheep; they were more restless than they had been all night... These highly-bred flocks of ours were inclined to be nervous, but I had learned that, at night especially, there was usually a cause. Sometimes they *felt* a coming danger or an enemy or some unusual circumstance long before any sense of sight or smell could have made them aware of it.

I lay there for perhaps five minutes more, when I heard a movement behind me. It was Marcus. He whispered to me as he passed, "Something is bothering the sheep; I'm going to take a look."

I rolled out of my blanket and stood. Above us on the hill, Alpheus had turned his face upward as though looking for something. It was an unlikely attitude of prayer for him.

The feeling of tension was still there; it was somehow in the air. I can't explain it well but the impression it left is clear to this day... I stretched, intending to follow Marcus. Simon, still in his blanket, coughed: small, ordinary things seem to stay in one's memory.

It was just at this moment that it happened. Marcus was on his way down the hill toward the flocks, Simon was still in his blanket, Alpheus was up on the small knoll. Two or three events occurred at once... A sudden movement, almost a small stampede, swept through the nearer sheep. As one, they moved away from the hill-slope. Marcus turned as Simon, from in back, cried, "Look! Look at Alpheus!"

Up on the little rise, the older shepherd was lying on his face in the cropped grass. All three of us rushed up toward him; I thought he had fainted... As we drew closer, Alpheus suddenly rose up on his knees and looked upward again. We got to him and paused uncertainly and it was Marcus who cried, "Listen!... Do you hear it?" And then the others were on *their* knees looking upward, Alpheus with a serene sort of joy written in his face, Marcus with puzzlement, and Simon with incredulous surprise. Only I remained standing.

I listened... There was nothing. The sheep below us were suddenly still. The silence was almost painful after the swift events of the past minutes.

I looked around at the others. Marcus was listening intently and then uncertainly, by turns. He would frown and look down, and then upward again... Simon, good old Simon, was gazing upward steadily; I started to speak to him and he waved me to silence almost savagely.

And Alpheus... Alpheus was gazing upward utterly attentive and yet in complete relaxation, oblivious to all about him. It was as though he himself had been transported to some far, high sphere, and only his physical body were there before us, motionless and full of a complete, compelling, winsome joy.

I can't put all of this into words very well. For months afterward I tried to explain to others, to friends, to anyone who would listen — just what had happened, and I invariably arrived at about this point and found myself at a loss for words...

As always, I'll try again, with you... On that cool early morning so long ago now, I stood there in the silence feeling — will you believe it? — feeling left out, alone. There was something real going on here; I had no doubt about that. I knew these men, these close working companions of mine, too well to believe that a sudden madness had struck each of them, all at once, all in the same moment of time.

I looked up... There were only the clear sky and the stars. I listened... There was only the sound of — stillness.

It was several minutes afterward when Alpheus, the first to move, rose to his feet.

"It's over," he said as he turned to walk back toward the embers of the fire. The others followed, I slowly, the last of all. I was feeling hurt, suddenly rejected from the group, and not a little confused. *What* was over?

We stood about the gently smoking embers in silence — for several minutes, I suppose. My pride kept me from saying anything, asking anything. And then I heard Alpheus' voice, half to himself.

"In a manger...a manger..." And then, aloud, "Well — we'd better go and see — or rather, you men go. I'll stay here with the sheep until you can relieve me."

It was Simon who spoke then, stoutly and not to be argued with. "No, Alpheus. I'm staying. You've got to go. It...well, you're expected to go. I'm staying."

Without another word, Alpheus turned away, reached for his cloak, and set out across the meadow in the moonlight toward the town. Marcus followed him, and after a brief moment of hesitation, I went too.

We walked in silence for some minutes across the slow upward slopes of the prairie and finally to the Bethlehem road. Before long, we were winding through the moonlit gardens of the first houses. No one had said a word, had offered the slightest bit of explanation. Finally, I spoke out of my hurt and aloneness.

"Alpheus, tell me. I saw nothing but the stars; I heard nothing except...silence. Tell me what happened."

The aging shepherd-scholar turned to me and put his hand on my shoulder as we walked. He said, "Do you remember the words of the prophet Isaiah about people who walked in darkness?"

I thought for a moment or two. My synagogue teachings were not as fresh as they had once been. And then I remembered; I recited the words slowly.

"The people that walked in darkness have seen a great light; they that dwelt in the land of the shadow of death, upon them hath the light shined."

For a full minute we walked in silence. Then,

"Yes, my son," said Alpheus. "That's it... Well, this — this is the time. The message came tonight — a baby, wrapped in swaddling clothes, and strangely, he will be found in — in a stable... And the music: didn't you hear the voices?"

I looked at him. His face in the moonlight was grave and serious; he meant what he had said. My bewilderment deepened, my sense of aloneness sharpened.

"I didn't hear anything," I said.

Then it was Marcus' turn to speak.

"I heard it — or I *think* I did. Now and again, when I stopped trying too hard and simply yielded myself to it, I heard — well, I thought it was singing..."

Then Alpheus said, "It was so loud that I thought my ears would be crushed under its impact..."

We walked for a few moments in silence.

"I didn't hear anything," I said again.

Alpheus' grip on my shoulder tightened. He spoke quietly. "The music was for those ears that were ready to hear it." He paused. Then, "The voice that spoke about the baby: Marcus didn't hear that. Yet, the voice was there; I'm convinced that it was there, and we'll find the child — you'll see... Simon heard the music clearly. Marcus heard it only indistinctly... It's a matter of where one stands, I think — how close to God..."

"And I didn't hear a thing," I said.

There was a brief silence, and then the old man said, "No, Son. You didn't hear a thing."

We went first to the commodious home of old Josephus, dividing town from prairie. His living quarters fronted several long stables with their numerous mangers, but he knew nothing about a new baby.

We turned into the town itself and Alpheus led us to the only inn. There are stables built into the caves that extend into the hill at the rear of the building; guests may shelter their beasts there.

The streets weren't empty even at this hour of the night. It was the year of Augustus' great census; no doubt you remember it. There were several Roman soldiers on patrol on our short little central street, and now and again a weary traveller would be seen searching for a place to pitch his small tent.

On our arrival, the innkeeper was asleep; the stableboy, though, rather excitedly blurted out the news that a baby had been born in one of the rear stables because the inn was full to bursting, and that he had been placed in a manger since there was no place else for him. It had happened only a couple of hours earlier; they had just finished making the mother comfortable. Perhaps, he said, we could see the baby...

With something like physical shock, I recalled Alpheus standing by the embers of the fire and talking to himself about — a manger! I felt a chill run up my back. I hadn't really argued inwardly over the things Alpheus had been saying to me during our journey into town. I had always found it impossible to argue with Alpheus. But verification still came with sudden impact... So he *had* heard what he felt were voices; he *had* been...spoken to.

The boy reappeared and beckoned us into the stables. We followed him past the rows of sleepy, odorous pack-animals and occasional saddle-horses into a small stable far in the rear. It hadn't been used for a long time, or else the boy had moved the animals out and worked rapidly. It was clean and quiet.

To tell you what we saw is easy; to share with you what we felt is probably impossible. I've tried on a number of occasions before, and somehow the words don't come...

What we saw was simply a young woman lying on some saddle-blankets over a mattress of quickly gathered hay. Within arm's reach of her was a small manger, and in it, resting deep in a hay-padded scarf, was a new baby. Standing close by, half protectively and half proudly, was a young man — clearly the father. There were a couple of women over against one wall; I assumed that they had been helping the young mother, making her comfortable. That was all.

It wasn't the strangeness of seeing a baby in a manger, only; after the other events of this night, my curiosity was hardly aroused. Nor was it only what Alpheus did, and finally the others of us...

I had been gazing at the baby, lost in my own thoughts, when I noticed that again, for the second time this night, I was the only one of us who was standing. Alpheus and Marcus were on their knees.

It wasn't embarrassment that brought me to my knees. It seemed — I can only tell you what I felt — it seemed somehow fitting to be kneeling there... It was the way one began to feel the longer he was in this quiet grotto-stable.

The baby looked like any other baby I've seen. He seemed pink and wrinkled from his recent birth-experience but also healthy and strong, and very deep in sleep. But — there was something else...

Have you ever sat alone of an evening in the field, dreaming or thinking? For the moment, you're far away from present surroundings. Then, suddenly, you *feel* the presence of someone else, and you look around, and there is one of your friends standing there. He hadn't said anything or made any noise, but you felt his presence... Have you?

That's the way it was in that stable. On the surface — ordinary things. But *below* the surface there was a presence; there was someone else there beside the people you could see.

I looked over at the young mother; she didn't look at her child quite the way that most new mothers do. Oh — there was the usual love and pride and pleasure and weariness and wistfulness and the rest. But if you watched her closely, you caught something else: there was a hint of awe there, something almost like fear in her eyes as she looked into the manger. There was an uncertainty, a wondering, a question; you *sensed* it as much as you *saw* it.

Alpheus was in quiet conversation with the father and then with the mother now and again; I couldn't hear much of what they were saying. Anyway, I was too busy savoring this strange new sensation, this odd feeling of a *presence*... I believe that it was in those moments that I became convinced of God's reality... Was it some of Alpheus' devotion that had transferred itself to me? Or was it the strangeness of this place and these conditions that somehow spoke to me?

Or was it — this child? Was the feeling of a Presence — this sense of visitation — was it because of this child?

At length, Alpheus knelt again one last time, and then he rose to his feet and we left the stable. We talked little on the way back. For some days thereafter I had no inclination to discuss what had happened to me. I think Alpheus knew, and he respected my need to think it through for myself.

As the weeks rolled by, I became able and even anxious to discuss the matter. Alpheus' conviction was that this child was to become the Messiah that would save Israel... He didn't mention this as a possibility: in his strong and quiet way he stated it as a fact.

I don't know whether Alpheus ever saw the child again. The parents with their infant son disappeared from Bethlehem quite suddenly some days later. Alpheus left us after several months to take a new position in the north, and it was shortly thereafter that we had news of his death. All of this was many years ago, years leading up to — yes, leading up to yesterday with the death of this young Galilean, coming out of Nazareth with his amazing message.

What I've been wondering is whether Alpheus ever knew about the sort of man this baby was to grow into...The Messiah?

I've been thinking ever since yesterday morning, when it dawned on me that this young preacher had been the baby of that almost-forgotten manger. *What would the Messiah really do?*

We Jews, the people of this land, have always imagined that the Messiah would come as a mighty military leader, haven't we? We're so prone to believe that it's our *might* that will save us.

But suppose we've been wrong... Suppose we've been feeding ourselves on a delusion in imagining that our tiny nation could ever build up the strength in arms to defeat mighty Rome... Suppose strength of arms isn't really the point... Suppose instead that this world and all of its history to come are ruled by *ideas* — by great acceptances on the part of large groups of people.

Suppose, for instance, that some of the convictions that this young preacher kept talking about *could* take hold of people. Suppose that someone would pick up the banner where he's been forced to drop it, and carry it on; he has a few followers, I understand. Suppose that this group should begin to grow...

Do you see how — perhaps — this might happen, and how in the end such a group might see the downfall even of mighty Rome?

I don't imagine things will come out that way. It's pretty unlikely, isn't it? People are so much more prone to take a spear in hand than they are to — how did he say it — *forgive*?

Well — they killed him this morning, and that's probably the end of it.

Yet, as I said at the beginning of this long story — I wonder... That baby in the manger: I met God there. Somehow, it happened to me... Could it have stopped with me? Why not others? Why not someday the world?

That's just a fancy, of course, and after all, this morning they crucified him. But — I wonder.

Chapter 2

Letters From Justin

On a dusty lower shelf in Section C-1 of the Palestinian Archives division of a scholarly library in Rome is an ancient file of letters written in good Latin script on ancient and dangerously desiccating parchment. The wax seals on several of the letters still bear enough of their original imprint to indicate that they were written by a centurion in the Roman army of occupation of Palestine early in the first century A.D.

A somewhat free translation, to best capture the true sense of the writer's intention, would read as follows.

* * *

My dearest Antonia,

Even in times of peace, the soldier's life is not easy. This irascible, this troublous people! They have not welcomed for a moment the cultural advantages which we offer them; they daily remind us of their preference for their ancient, half-civilized ways of life. Though we would do much for them if they would allow us, the fact is that we are constantly on our own defense; any one of us foolish enough to venture forth alone may well find himself face down in the dusty street with a knife in his back.

Under usual circumstances I wouldn't have minded all of this, of course. In fact, it helps the hours to roll more rapidly by until the day when I shall take ship again for Rome, and you... The excitement, the hidden danger — you know I would not have minded.

But this last assignment... It seems that the Caesar, blessed be his name, has decreed that all of the people of our eastern colonial possessions shall be counted; he wants a census of them —

as if one could go into any of these local oriental markets and count all of its flies. In very fact, my lord the Emperor knows not what he asks.

In view of this, I have received new orders. I must leave Joppa's pleasant wharves and beaches for the capital. To be sent to Jerusalem would have been bad enough in itself. But to be ordered in addition into the temporary service of such a provincial petty monarch as this Herod — is almost too bitter a pill to swallow. The man is without honor and a butcher to boot, if the stories one hears about him are true.

We have been warned that a large congestion of the population is expected in this Jerusalem-Bethlehem area during the days of the census. It is the rule in this strange land that to be legally counted, each male must return to the particular place of his family roots, his native soil, there to be enrolled. Most of the time, of course, he must bring wife and family with him. So — the influx of travellers to the capital will doubtless exceed that of any event in its past.

The Jerusalem district is historic in its way. It was the seat of this people's prime legendary hero, one "King David," and it proves to be a particularly sensitive place in which to maintain a military presence. Several of us have been ordered into temporary service here, to strengthen the regular resident forces.

However, as to my added duty: It appears that this petty monarch Herod enjoys the trust of no one — not even of his own people; he has murdered too many of them in cold blood. This is the man on whom I'm to keep a wary eye during the coming days. Outwardly, I shall be under his command as a courtesy — as a sort of Roman delegate to his personal forces. Privately, I'm to spy on the man and report periodically to area Headquarters. I shall have to obey his orders for the period of my assignment, of course; I'll obey him with great care, in fact, so that I shall give no cause for suspicion.

Farewell, Beloved, for the moment. By the time you have received this, I shall be thoroughly established in the good graces and at the good table of King Herod. Pray me luck!

Your devoted Justin.

* * *

My Antonia,

You will know that I have been in the palace of this petty ruler for a fortnight. It is a palatial life indeed — too luxurious, too artificial. Herod "the Great," as he is misnamed, has built a new residence atop an abrupt hill which the natives in their unmanageable tongue call "Jebel Fureidis" — or Little Paradise Mountain. His dwelling is a combination of palace and fortress, and it is filled stiflingly, day and night, with as dissolute a crowd of wastrels as one could easily find.

Herod himself is an Idumean usurper, the grandson of one who was a mere priest in the temple at Ascalon. On this slender thread the king hangs his worthless pretension to what, in its small way, is a really historic throne. It reaches back far beyond any of our Roman histories; not surprisingly, the local people are intensely proud of it — and smolderingly resentful of this brute of a usurper who, with Roman support, continues on as monarch.

Due, no doubt, to Herod's questionable right to the throne, he is intensely jealous of it; he is thrown literally into a tantrum if any question concerning it reaches his ears. He has put to death several who have cast even the slightest suspicion on him, including his brother-in-law, the young nobleman Aristobulus, whom he caused to be drowned in pretended sport before his very eyes. In a fit of passion he ordered the strangulation of the only woman whom, it is rumored, he ever loved — the strikingly beautiful Asmonean princess Mariamne... Yes, she was his wife...

In any event, such is the man whom I have been assigned to serve — and to watch. Wish me well with your love!

All of mine you have... Justin

* * *

My Antonia,

It is not easy to put into words, words that you will understand, an event that has recently occurred. I've written the beginning of this letter several times to you over the past few days, only to cease writing, defeated.

It all began as a routine matter — such an ordinary thing...

In my recent word to you I described in some detail the character of this petty King Herod whom I have been assigned to watch. All of this may help you to understand Herod's reaction some days ago when word came that a trio of visiting nobles from the eastern deserts wished an audience with him. They would arrive mid-afternoon, and there was quite a fluster of preparation for their coming and quite an occasion was made of it — until they stated their purpose. They sought information about a young king who had just been born, or was about to be, as they put it, in this vicinity.

It was instructive — and amusing — to watch Herod's face change expression. At first he was obviously startled, then for a moment terribly afraid, and then he recovered his crafty urbanity.

I should say to you that Herod is not a brilliant man, but neither is he a fool. It was clear that he had heard nothing about such a birth, but he parried by asking his visitors to wait in an anteroom while he conferred with his advisors. The visiting nobles retired, and immediately Herod's manner changed.

Loudly he ordered a lackey to summon the temple authorities, and by the time these worthies arrived on the scene, Herod was in a towering rage. He demanded to know *what* young prince had been born, where and when, and why he had not been told. The motley group of advisors quite naturally protested their innocence at length, whereupon Herod attacked them with his vitriol all over again.

This went on for several long minutes, until a youthful minor temple authority by the name of Caiaphus suggested that they search the "Scriptures" — a written account of ancient Jewish history that is held in great veneration by the people. This young cleric had obviously prepared himself: he opened a large scroll that he had been carrying under his arm, wrinkled his forehead in great studiousness, and then pointed out that the prophets more than once had spoken of a King to be born one day in Bethlehem. Anxious for an excuse to withdraw, the other dignitaries vigorously endorsed this prophecy, and then disappeared.

Herod wasted no time. Calling for the visitors to return into the audience room, he directed them to Bethlehem without more ado. He is a superstitious man, and it was clear to those of us who looked on that he was more concerned about the matter than his advisors had been.

It is at this point, my dearest, that you will see why I have related all of this long story to you... Immediately upon the departure of the visiting nobles, Herod beckoned to me. In some surprise, I heard him direct me to follow the "Magi" — noblemen-scholars really, men who study the heavens — to follow them at a discreet distance, and to report back to him upon their findings. He had also asked *them* to report back, but he wasn't sure they would do so.

I was loathe to go for a number of reasons, particularly my desire not to let the King out of my sight; clearly, I was being sent on a wild goose-chase. However, I chose not to arouse his suspicions; to avoid further complication, I took to my favorite mount and picked up the trail. It wasn't difficult to do, even in the fading light: the grubby, rutted little town of Bethlehem is only five Roman miles south of Jerusalem, and the easterners were in no hurry as they swayed along atop their ridiculous camels.

It had been late in the day when our strange company left Little Paradise Mountain — the three eastern noblemen with their extensive retinue of servants and pack-animals, and I, alone and at a discreet distance, keeping my Sejanus at an unaccustomed walk. Not happy with the pace, he whinnied and tossed his head.

It was soon night — a clear, cold evening. The stars were unusually bright, I remember, or it may simply be that in the intervening days my whole memory of the thing has been unbalanced by two amazing discoveries that have marked that memorable night indelibly for me.

We must have been half way to Bethlehem when I saw the star...

My Dearest, I don't know how to convey to you what I feel about all of this. Perhaps I won't have to lead your understanding. Perhaps our love ties us in such a sensitive bond that already *you* have been feeling what *I* have been feeling.

I wouldn't have said such a thing to you heretofore, would I? I wonder if you're finding my words surprising or unnerving...

Sejanus had been calmer over the recent minutes; the night was growing colder. I was conscious suddenly that my slow-moving quarry had come to a stop. From a small hill I watched them — the three noblemen-scholars atop their tall, shapeless beasts pointing upward and talking together, quietly, without excitement... Then they moved ahead.

I looked up.

Antonia, I'm convinced that it was there — a star, brighter than those around it... I have thought about it constantly since; I have lived my memory of it over and over again, wondering even if this strange people about me have affected my mind.

Respected astrologers do tell us, of course, that stars come and go in the heavens, shining brightly for a season and then fading; they know no mortal reason why. Surely no sorcerer can exercise his magic upon stars! At any rate, I know only that in this instance, the star was there.

I'm still not sure how it happened that the real reason for the visit of these nobles suddenly dawned on me, there on the road, alone: these scholars were in Judea *because* of that star. One might almost say that they had been following it. It wasn't that the star moved, of course; it was surely quite normal, except for its surprising brightness.

It was rather as though the star were a sign, a signal...

I'm too familiar with the appearance of the Judean sky at night not to know that the star was new. Coupled with this certainty is a strange tradition here in the east — I've run across it several times — that the appearance of a new star heralds the birth of a king, perhaps near at hand, perhaps at a distance.

So it was that I knew why the Magi were here. This star had moved them to come in search... As I jogged along, I looked at the star again and again; it was surely no figment of the imagination: it was there. Men who know about such things have recorded many strange occurrences in the heavens; nature seems to allow them. Whatever its origin, though, to the Magi this star had spelled a divine message... In spite of myself, I began to take a new interest in my journey and in what might be found at the end of it.

Why or how it was that the Magi associated the star with Judea and allowed it to "lead" them here, is not yet clear to me. What is clear, my Antonia, is that these travellers under a star found what they were looking for. They went away satisfied and justified. Their journey had accomplished its purpose.

I can imagine your amazement, my Dearest. Do I mean that they truly found a king — the king for which they searched?

We're now at the fountainhead of this whole experience. It's what has had me in the toils of mental conflict, a kind of emotional tension, ever since. There is something afoot here that is apart from all of my familiar patterns of thought. Am I writing foolishness? Are you laughing at me as you read? Please — hear me out...

We entered the little hamlet of Bethlehem, Sejanus and I, on the heels of the straggling retinue of the easterners. The three nobles were pausing in the middle of the crowded street, surrounded by weary census-travellers; they were uncertain of their next move.

I suspected that they were looking for a palace of some kind, fit for the birth of a king. Nothing in Bethlehem, except for the usual sprawling inn, has more than two rooms. I understood their perplexity. I was familiar with the town as they were not, however, and I hastened to the inn. I knew that my noble travellers would come to it shortly; there was simply nowhere else to go.

I walked behind my mount as the boy led him to a stall. The stables were very crowded; in poor Latin the boy apologized for the situation as he began to curry the horse slowly with a rough comb. He was irritatingly slow at his task; I could have comforted Sejanus for the night in half the time myself. I occupied the interval by going over Sejanus's bridle straps and engaging in small talk. There seemed nothing else to do. Everything was full, the boy said, to the bursting point... A woman had even had to come into one of the inner stables earlier in the week to have her baby.

I was kneeling, examining a weakened saddle-loop, hardly listening to the boy's prattle. It was a full half-minute before the import of what he had said broke upon me. I rose quickly.

"A baby," I said. "Where is it now?"

He motioned with his arm in the direction of the inn building itself. "The next day we moved them into a room; people come and go so fast in this census. The keeper said it was only the human thing to do, what with the mother and the new baby and —" I left him staring after me.

It wasn't hard to find the right place; a curious group from the street was huddled at the doorway into a small room. I spoke quietly and they scattered before me; then, in the doorway, I stopped.

My three noblemen from the Jordan deserts had somehow passed me during the delay with my horse, because here they were. What is more important, they had come to the end of their quest... My Antonia, how can I help you grasp and believe what I saw with my own eyes?

The Magi, dressed in their full finery, were kneeling — yes, kneeling — on the floor of the dusty little room, offering rich gifts to a tiny new baby that lay sleeping, of all places, in a small manger that the innkeeper had apparently moved in from one of his stables. To one side, on a simple cot, lay the child's mother, and standing near the manger, half protectively, was the young father. They were humble peasants, and in the few words that were initially passed between the young man and the visitors I caught a familiar bit of Galilean guttural.

The star, and then this scene... For a moment, frightened, I wondered if my mind were breaking under the strain of a pressure far beyond my understanding. I put out a hand to lean against the doorsill.

The three easterners had now turned away from the manger. There was quiet conversation between one of them and the young father. Another was on one knee as he spoke with the mother. I suppose most of an hour passed as I stood there watching and listening, struggling to control an unaccustomed inner confusion that was almost fear.

Then I saw that the Magi were preparing to depart. Quickly I stepped back into the crowded little hallway; the curiosity-bound group from the street had stayed by to see how it would all end.

Quite unconscious of me but with a strange expression of — what shall I say — exultation on their faces, the easterners passed on down the hallway and through the outer door. The crowd streamed after them, completely incurious about the child; babies were common enough, even in Bethlehem. It was the richly dressed foreigners that had drawn the crowd.

Then, inexplicably, I found myself hurrying after the aristocratic visitors. Outside, across the square enclosure of the stable-yard, I saw them; I pushed my way through the pressing crowd.

Breathless, I said, "Do not return to Herod. Tell him nothing. He is a dangerous man."

Antonia, I don't know why I did this. It made nonsense of my assignment to spy on these men. The whole affair seems veiled in confusion as I think back on it.

The three of them turned to look at me, not with respect but with a politely controlled curiosity. One of them spoke in oddly accented Latin in deference to my Roman uniform.

"Have no fear of your Herod," he said. "None shall harm that child. Where he goes, the great God goes with him." That was all. Before I could recover myself, they were gone in the crowd.

I must have stood there for many minutes, only dimly conscious of the throng of travellers and pack animals that milled

about me even at that hour of the night. Then, realizing only one thing clearly, which was that I had carelessly made myself known to my quarry and so had failed in my responsibility to spy on them, I returned to the stall assigned to my still wakeful Sejanus. I threw the saddle on with my own hands and rode forth into the night.

Since my return, Herod has been fuming about the failure of the Magi from the east to report back to him. I simply reported that I had not seen anything resembling a young king — which was true — and have said nothing else.

There... I have told you everything, just as it happened. If my conduct seems strange to you, be assured that it has seemed doubly strange to me... All of my love.

Justin

* * *

My Antonia,

Only a single week has passed since my last word to you. I am grateful that our regular shipping from the harbor of Joppa allows such frequent word to be exchanged between us. I write again to say that the child of Bethlehem, unbelievably, has crossed my path a second time.

I mentioned to you earlier that Herod was angry that no message had come to him from the three nobles from the east. More than this, he has been deeply suspicious and frightened; his superstitions about the threat of a baby king to his throne are almost more than his sanity will allow.

Yesterday morning he called me in and ordered me to take a detachment of his regulars and proceed to Bethlehem. There — you will be deeply shocked at the horror of this, Antonia, but it is the truth — there we were to search out every male child two years old and under and do away with it. Herod had few of the facts, but he did know that the child he sought was an infant; in this strange culture, a child is so regarded until the age of two years.

I refused point blank to obey Herod's order. It was a dangerous thing to do, Antonia, but there is a limit to what one can stomach. Personally I am safe, of course, as an officer of the Roman army. Whether the king has become suspicious of my presence in his palace, I have yet to discover.

Herod's next move was the expected one. He ordered a detachment of his own men, on pain of death if they failed, to carry out his command. But I was ahead of him...

Anticipating that he would do this very thing, I had taken my leave on a pretext and made straight for the Bethlehem road.

I gave Sejanus his head this time, and it was hardly forty minutes before I was galloping up the dusty main street of the town. The census-date had passed, and with the precipitous drop in trade, the young couple was allowed to remain in its small room for the mother's first days of recovery. I found them without difficulty, stood only briefly in the door, and entered. I told them of Herod's order.

The young mother looked at me with a question in her eyes. There was a silence, and then, "Why did you come to tell us?" she asked.

It was only then that I realized that she had never seen me. My uniform and military insignia seemed incongruous in that mud-walled little room. I looked at her. She was holding her child easily, accustomed to him now. Briefly I told her the history of the past days, how I had advised the Magi to avoid Herod, and the petty king's latest move. She smiled.

"Now you are saving the life of my child a second time," she said. Then, quite simply, "Why are you doing it?"

I realize now, thinking back upon it, that it was not as though she herself were curious. The question was asked as though she wanted me to turn inward, to give myself an answer...almost — to make a confession.

I wasn't ready for this. I couldn't — or wouldn't — put an answer into words. A baby; a mere infant. What peculiar magnetism had somehow reached out of the door of an ancient mud-walled little room to move me so tellingly? Something here goes beyond the natural, visible things of earth that until now have set the boundaries of what I will accept as real and permanent.

Strange words for me to be writing, my Antonia. I have never been near enough to the child even to touch him. The beginning edge of this, though, was in my mind later as I was helping the mother into the saddle of their riding-animal.

Antonia, I am frightened. An enemy on the battlefield I can handle; I understand the boundaries of that sort of confrontation. But there is something in all of this that is beyond my ken. I can only say that there is a magnetism here which comes from beyond or outside of my experience. It is unnatural, in the sense that that which is natural to me I can describe or at least choose or reject. Perhaps it all springs from what I can only call a beckoning presence, something personal which calls me personally. I can describe it in no other way at the moment.

What if this child ever lives to become a man? What if this strange sense of a presence that has somehow exercised itself upon me is someday coupled with the intelligence of a mature mind? Such a one could destroy the world with his power — or save it...

As I mentioned above, the beginning edge of this train of thought was in my mind as I bade the peasant couple to hurry, and as I went myself for their stabled pack-animal. In the space of less than thirty minutes, I was riding slowly beside them on the road southward out of Bethlehem. I satisfied myself that they would be safe as they travelled, and then I turned back northward alone. In what followed in Bethlehem at Herod's orders, unpleasant as it was, I know that the young couple with their infant were not apprehended.

The child lives, somewhere to the south. I shall never see him again. Whatever and whoever he is, the matter is closed, and in most waking moments I am relieved. There come nights of sleeplessness, to be sure, when my restless mind harks back to a mud-walled room in an ancient inn, struggling for an answer that somehow does not come. Perhaps in all of this, you are perceiving a pattern in the cloth which is evading me... How I long to talk it through with you!

My love to you.

Justin

* * *

My Antonia,

As you must be only too aware, two months have come and gone since my last word to you. There is little to tell you, except that Herod's anger and his trust of me both grow cooler. We have little to say to one another, and I am merely biding my time until I am relieved of this post.

I have not advanced myself in this assignment, my Love. In fact, since my experience with the strange child in Bethlehem I have been a failure from both the diplomatic and the military points of view: I have failed to hold the confidence of the king. Colonial headquarters is not pleased.

I have heard a rumor that I am to be assigned to Rhinocolura, an evil little town on the Palestinian-Egyptian border far to the south; I suppose it's by way of military punishment... My deepest hope is that it will not too much delay my return to you.

All of my love is yours... Justin

* * *

There is only one more letter in the file that is of interest to us now. It is dated by the Roman calendar some seven months later.

* * *

My Antonia,

I am writing this from Tiberias. It has been almost like coming home again to return to the lovely shores of Galilee. And — my Love, for the first time I have found the place to which I could happily bring you as my bride, God willing.

God willing! There, you see: already I am falling into the speech and the habits of thought of this land. The people here worship only one God, whom they conceive to be the creator and sustainer of all things... Seriously, the idea is not so unlikely as you might think on first hearing of it.

One part of my news for you is that I shall be taking ship homeward, to Rome and you. Yes, my Love. The day is not far distant.

But — Antonia, I must return...to this land. This is the second part of my news. I hope and I trust that you will be with me, and knowing you as I do, I believe I shall not come alone.

As I wrote you, Rhinocolura was a rough and difficult place. I hated it enthusiastically and counted the very hours until my relief.

Finally the blessed day came, and before noon Sejanus was saddled and nervously chewing his bit. I looked one last time at the small border station on the bank of the river. There was a group of travellers coming from the Egyptian deserts to the west. I turned away — and then whirled around to stare at them more closely. My eyes hadn't deceived me: among the travellers were the peasant of Bethlehem, his very young wife and their child... I don't remember pondering the matter; it didn't strike me as coincidence. Strangely, it seemed at the moment the most natural occurrence in the world.

Of course I hurried to them, silenced a young officer who was being difficult about their crossing the border, and greeted them. They remembered, and their eyes shone with gratitude and genuine pleasure. It was the loveliest moment in all my long months in this arid, neglected border station.

They had heard of Herod's death, and they were returning to their homeland. I had to tell them that Archelaus, Herod's younger son, had been appointed to reign in his father's stead, that his choice on the part of Rome had been a tragic one, and that already he was well on the way toward outperforming his father's record as a vicious brute and murderer. It was unpleasant news to have to bring them, but it was the truth.

I'll never forget the look of panic on the young father's face. He gazed back across the Egyptian desert, and he didn't have to put his thoughts into words.

Antonia, once again, as so often before in this whole amazing adventure, I found myself speaking words that didn't seem to be my own but rather put into my mouth by another. Yet, at the time they seemed sensible and right once I heard myself speaking them, and I was prepared to live by what I was saying.

"No," I said as the young peasant turned his eyes back to mine. "Listen to me. You're Galilean; I know it by your speech. I myself have been ordered to Tiberias, leaving at once. Let me — let me go with you. We'll turn east at Gaza; we'll round the southern end of the Salt Sea to Areopolis and return north on the eastern side of the Jordan. You'll be safe with me and out of the reach of Archelaus."

The young mother, her lovely child in her arms, looked at me and asked the same question she had asked on another occasion.

"This is the third time you have saved the life of my son. Why are you doing it?"

Antonia, I gave her the only answer I have been able to give myself.

"I *must* do it," I said. "I'm not able to tell you why — the reason isn't at all clear to me... I can't give you more of an answer than that."

Then it was the young man who spoke. "Your company will mean much to us. We will go with you — and our thanks..."

I went with them all the way to Nazareth, my Love, and then returned eastward here to the shore of the lake.

Antonia, I have wondered so constantly over these many months whether you are understanding and feeling into the strange experience I've lived through. You are a woman, and oftentimes a woman grasps the meaning of things of the heart more quickly and clearly than does a man.

This child... Only a babe in arms he is now, with peasant parents, and yet I say to you with all the conviction of which I'm able that a power and a presence work through him... If one day he does become a ruler of people, I have the strange certainty that his rule will be a new thing, not a matter that the world has seen before, or understood.

When that occurs, I must be a part of it, Antonia. I must. I know that you will not ply me with questions that I cannot yet answer. But — Tiberias is beautiful, my Love, and Nazareth is not far distant. This is a home-loving people. We shall be near to his growing up, and one day we shall understand.

Will you take my hand and walk into uncertainty with me, with only my strange sureness to guide us — my conviction that the outcome will be glorious?

Antonia, mighty Rome with all of her power may have at last met her match... Mark my words: Rome has met her conqueror.

All of my love to you.

Justin

Chapter 3

Joseph The Father

One of the most central but least noted figures of the first Christmas is that of Joseph, the husband of Mary. A largely uneducated peasant, he showed remarkable reserve and acceptance in a situation of undoubted personal difficulty. Joseph was a man of great wisdom.

Translating from a dusty papyrus manuscript in somewhat cribbed Aramaic and doing it as accurately as possible, forming sentences where there were none before and supplying necessary words where they had simply been omitted in the original, I am able to share with you a record of some of his experiences, written apparently very close to the time of his own early death. His opening words suggest how intuitively he related to his son... He begins thus:

I do not believe that most people will understand my son. Folk of calm and temperate judgement will be puzzled by him, often to the point of rejection. I've been learning, however, that calmness and temperateness, while they are valuable qualities of mind for much of life, sometimes stand one in very poor stead.

I do not believe, in fact, that most people will receive my son for what I have come to know him to be. For this reason, and also because of the recurring cough which is sapping my strength in the prime of my life, I have determined to write down all that memory will supply of my years with him. It has been — and this surprises me in thinking about it — it has been almost fifteen years ago now. It seems, on the contrary, like yesterday, so constantly have I lived and wrestled with the recollection of it.

You will be aware already that I have written very little in my years of life. I have lived always by my hands, not by any creative power of my mind. What I shall chronicle here will be simply done; indeed, it may seem to you crude and inept. If so, I make no apology; I am a carpenter. I am a fashioner of benches, not words.

I have said that few people will understand my son. More, I am sure that his way in life will be hard. I can only hope that he will not be without friends and some who love him when I am no longer with him. I hope, too, that a knowledge of his task and of God's near presence will be as clear someday to him as it has become to me.

For all of these reasons, then, I am writing down before it is too late this brief history — the history of his beginning. Before it is too late, I say... It is strange that a mere recurrent coughing can squeeze out a man's mortal life. However, it has happened before in our village, and to me it is now happening. I have — a year, perhaps months.

Afterward it will be the responsibility of Jesus to care for his mother and the younger ones of the family. I have no fears; he has shown marked ability with the tools of our trade, and in my absence he will shoulder the full responsibility of serving not only our village but the environs as well. He has been working this morning on a chair, a small one for one of the neighbor children, and his dexterity surprises me as I have been watching him across the work table. Yes, he will be able to provide...

Bitter to me is the realization that I shall not be able to share what must lie ahead, share the burden of it. I have lived long enough to know that there is travail in store for one who habitually remembers his own needs and desires last — if only because the man or woman on the street so misunderstands this turn of mind and spirit.

Be aware that such *is* Jesus's way; in the family circle, we have become so used to it that it seems the natural thing to expect from him. I am not equipped to make judgement of my son's native gifts, though our village rabbi seems proud of his attainments. I do know, however, that my daily dealings with my son are with one who is completely selfless.

I should add that there is nothing abject about him, though the ordinary eye may see this in Jesus. In his younger years I often watched him at play with the other children, and though he was quick to take for himself the more unpopular positions in the games, his fellows frequently forced him into responsible ones. He had their admiration, although they — and he — would be the last ones to recognize the fact.

I am concerned that you do not understand me as merely a doting father. In fact, the burden of what I have to relate has little to do with my eldest as he now is. I have set my hand to write down with truth and no embellishment the simple facts surrounding his birth. I make no apology for what may seem to you quite illogical and full of question, utter fancy perhaps. I am writing so that the facts may not be completely lost and forgotten. No others may be moved to write of him, and the world may not accept him or remember him after he has gone...

The story begins with my betrothal to Mary, the daughter of a market-keeper in our town. We had known one another from childhood, were often together, and I'm sure it was the assumption of not a few in our community that one day we would be wed.

I write of all of this quite calmly now, but it was a matter for anything but calmness then. I can remember our long walks together on warm evenings, our meals together in the home of her parents or mine, our doing the many simple things that young lovers do. I particularly resented our forced distance during synagogue worship — I sitting with the men, of course, and she with the women.

It was impossible for us to be married as early as was then ordinarily assumed, partly because there had been a series of lean and dry years in Galilee and my earnings as a carpenter came with difficulty.

I was in my mid-twenties, she a bit younger, when a cycle of better rains came and with it better times for all of Galilee. Our betrothal was made public. I hope it is not fatuous for me to say that my bride-to-be was an uncommonly lovely woman. As for the fortunes of life, Mary could have done better than the village carpenter, as I'm sure the town gossip had it. However, having known one another always, we found a natural fitness in preparing to take each other as man and wife.

This is the point at which my narrative may begin to tax your credulity. I am wondering as I write what you, as my reader, may think about...dreams.

There are those folk who see dreams as quite meaningless, mere reflections, as in a mirror, of our lives while awake. There are others who are certain that all dreams are sent of God, or of Satan, to influence us one way or the other in our wakeful decisions. I must presume that either of these is possible, and I leave it to the philosopher or the rabbi to decide between them. I can only say that in my own life there have been a small handful of instances where dreams have influenced me greatly.

In the course of time, word came that the Caesar, who in that year was named Augustus, had decreed a census and taxation for many of the Roman colonies. Our Palestine was among these. As was the ancient Palestinian custom, it was further decreed that each male should return to the city in which his family line had its roots, there to complete his registration.

This would in itself have been inconvenient enough, as all who endured it know that it was, but for me it had an additional complication. Mary and I had now been married for some months, she was with child, and she had not long.

I must admit that at first I had not wanted this child. I was pointedly ungracious when she informed me of the situation. My wife had not been in the best of health at the beginning of our married life, and — certain other elements of the matter bothered me greatly.

I was slow to understand. I readily accept that fact now, and there are still parts of it all that I have never wholly understood. During the weeks, though, of what I fear was a petulant sort of resentment on my part, my wife never once lost either her temper or her charm. And — one night I had a dream...

I have said a word about dreams already; they may be meaningless or highly significant, as you will. I suspect that what they are depends centrally on one's own sense of need and the set of his or her mind. I make no attempt to explain the dream I experienced; I only know that I awoke from it in peace. It is elusive now as all dreams are afterward, although I must have discussed it with my wife; particular anxieties of mine concerning her were a part of it: that much I recall clearly.

Be this as it may, as I have said I awoke from my dream in peace. It was as though something or someone had spoken to me to reassure me; I knew, just as surely as it is given to us to know certain things on this earth, that all would be well where the coming birth was concerned.

Weeks passed, and then there came upon us the time for the census I have mentioned. The date and place of it for my tribe of David were exact and unchangeable, and it would be very close to the time our child could be expected. I tried to keep from Mary my concern and my sense of the injustice of the decree; I knew that I might well be absent when the child was born. One day I voiced this to Mary, and she looked at me with some surprise.

"But — didn't you know?" she said. "I'm going with you."

I blinked at her in amazement. It was a five-day trip of hard travel southward to Bethlehem for an able man, considerably longer for a man and wife even under the best of conditions. Mary's was hardly the best of conditions.

I considered the situation in silence. Perhaps I could ask for a place of registry nearer to Galilee — but even as the thought occurred, I rejected it. My presenting myself at the ancient seat of the house of David was required, and I knew it.

Mary broke the silence. "Joseph," she said, "some months ago you told me about a dream you had had... Well, a dream came to me one night, too — before yours came. I might not have believed in mine until you spoke of yours," here she looked away, "...and as you told me of it you changed: you became my loving companion again... You gave me strength, Joseph, to trust my dream."

I suppose I merely stared at her. When she spoke again, she was seeking to reassure me; in actual fact, she added to my confusion.

"You know what our Scriptures say about the birthplace of the Messiah that is to come one day. Centuries ago the prophets spoke of it — Bethlehem Ephratha... Joseph, don't think me a complete fool, but I do want to go with you. You see," — here Mary paused in embarrassment, and then she summoned the courage to say what was on her heart — "it may be the will of God that our baby should be born in Bethlehem... Perhaps you'll call it simply a woman's whim, but — Joseph, I'm going with you."

Mary was hardly in a condition to travel to the end of our town's main street and back, much less the twenty-six leagues that lay ahead to Bethlehem. I could not dispute her, though — perhaps because of the way her words had affected me. Each of us had experienced a dream, the two of them somehow fitting together, as hand and glove. I realized as I pondered the matter during the next days, that it was not the unexpectedness of Mary's words that had shocked me; it was quite the opposite. The realization grew that I had been *waiting* to hear them. In the depths of my mind somewhere, hidden by daily surface concerns, had been the unspoken and surely unreasoned idea that our child *should* be born in Bethlehem. Mary's words had forced the matter up into my consciousness; they had the effect almost of physical impact.

In the succeeding days, I found it impossible to do other than help Mary prepare for our trip. I was able to borrow a small pack-animal so that Mary could ride upon our own mule. As the day for our departure drew near, though, my tension grew rapidly. It would have been a demanding enough trip for me alone, and I knew that the traveltime might well be doubled under the circumstances. Most frightening of all was the thought that the child might come while we were on the way; it was an unpleasant prospect, and I couldn't shake it off. Meanwhile, Mary went about her preparations with serenity and composure.

The weather was cool on the midmorning of our departure. Mary was calm, but it was to be a nerve-wracking time for me — all eight days of it. We went down the narrow road eastward out of Nazareth that leads onto the north-south lakeshore highway which the Romans built some decades ago, and then we turned southward toward the holy city. After a day's travel we crossed the Jordan and then continued southward down the east bank of the river.

To my surprise, despite my own constant inner tension it was on the whole an easy journey. Mary was uncomplaining in spite of what must often have been genuine discomfort, and she took a real interest in the passing scene. She enjoyed people, and though most of our fellow travellers could move more rapidly than we, often they would fall in with us for a little distance to enjoy my wife's easy conversation.

We spent nights under the stars, but on the evening of the sixth day, I obtained a simple room in the small inn at Beeroth; it was clear that Mary's time was near at hand. I was hiding my feeling of panic very poorly, but Mary smiled at me and told me not to worry. She eventually dropped off into an easy sleep and slept most of the night through; I know, because I spent it pacing our room.

The next morning Mary insisted on continuing our journey; on entering Jerusalem's Damascus Gate in late afternoon, we hardly paused as we hurried on southward through the city's winding streets and teeming crowds.

The final two leagues to Bethlehem were accomplished somehow, though the memory of them is a jumble to me. Mary was determined to finish our journey, though there were more than a few times when I know that she was on the verge of stopping and having me hail passing travellers for help.

We arrived late in the evening to find that there is only one inn in little Bethlehem. Mary was too exhausted to talk as she sat upon our small beast, and only a whiteness around her mouth gave evidence of her physical and mental tension.

The inn courtyard was full of people, some of them hurrying to and fro and all of them talking loudly and laughing. After some difficulty I located the innkeeper. He informed me in a tired voice that the inn was full to overflowing, that he had been saying the same thing to travellers since mid-afternoon, and that he hoped the pressure of this senseless census would soon be over.

I have never, I think, felt so friendless and alone. I started to turn away, and then I swallowed my pride and told him our plight.

Immediately he looked concerned. He asked me to wait, and he was gone for only a handful of minutes. Then he returned and offered to have a place cleared in the inner stables — some quiet corner, he said; in other crowded times he had put travellers there, and it would be better than no shelter at all. I accepted gratefully and we followed him into the stables.

The next hours are far from clear in my memory. There were suddenly women present who pushed me out into the night. I walked awhile; it was beautifully clear. The stars were unusually bright — I recall thinking that, consciously; it was as though all nature were about to break forth in song. Such musings were hardly unusual in expectant fathers, I reflected...

It was then, I believe, that I began through my weariness to think through my wife's desire to reach Bethlehem... The Messiah — that was what she had in mind: just a whim, of course...or was it? What had implanted the idea in the first place? Why should she have thought about it at all; after all, childbirth is hardly an uncommon experience for a woman.

With a start, I recalled my odd feeling of — what had it been — expectedness, a strange sort of familiarity? Down in the deep recesses of thought had something of the same germ of an idea been born in me? Whatever the reason, I knew and had to admit to myself that Mary's words about Bethlehem and the Messiah had not seemed outlandish to me.

I shook my head to bring back some sanity. This train of thought was less than sensible — not a little ridiculous, in fact... I turned back toward the inn, walking faster now.

When I arrived at the stable, all was over. I entered quickly at the invitation of a woman whom I assumed had been waiting for me.

Mary was lying on an improvised bed of several robes thrown over a hasty pile of hay. She smiled a little as I entered and took her hand; in less than a minute she was asleep.

Then I thought of the baby. I looked in question at the woman who had admitted me; she pointed to a manger close by and then she disappeared.

I am not rich in words. I can only tell you what I felt as I first gazed into the manger that they had lined with hay and covered with a simple saddle-cloth. There lay a child, and he was fast asleep.

I suppose every father since the beginning of time has jousted with onsetting tears as he first looks upon his newborn child.

Pride, and a quick-springing love and a sense of protectorship — these are all a part of it. But here there was something more...

I thought much about this later. I found that I could neither cope with nor understand the odd and frightening sense that was deeper even than my own feeling for him: the child was mine, and yet I knew that he belonged to another, or to the world — perhaps to both. He was just a baby, asleep. I knew then, though, and I've thought often upon it since, that I didn't wholly own him in the usual fatherly sense; he would always belong to another.

What I can only call a signal was given to me later in the evening. Some shepherds came to call. There were three of them, rough fellows directly from the fields. They came straight in with little ceremony, as though they knew exactly where to look; they stood around the manger gazing down. Then — I could understand this, curiously, because I had felt the same impulse — they knelt in the dust of that stable. They, too, sensed the involvement of someone or something beyond what was visible there in the manger.

After awhile they departed, first speaking briefly with Mary; I went to the edge of the courtyard with them. On the way they told me — please remember that I'm telling only the simple facts of what happened, as exactly as memory allows — the shepherds informed me that they had been *told* of the birth of my son — by a message from God, as they described it. They were quiet and controlled about this, although one could see that they had been deeply excited; in honesty, I must say that after all that had assaulted my senses this night, their news held little surprise for me.

I returned and stood for a long while looking down into the improvised cradle. Could it be...could it? Here was no palace, no rich surroundings, no promise of arms and armor... The Messiah? Yet God's way of working can be strange indeed.

My train of thought turned to Mary. What of her conviction about the possibility of this, long beforehand; what of my strange sense of familiarity, of recognition when she had voiced her thoughts? Overarching it all was the birth in Bethlehem which could so easily have come to pass along the way, and the oddly fitting news the shepherds had brought with them.

I stood for awhile longer, and then I knelt in prayer with my forehead resting against that rude manger-cradle. Finally, deeply exhausted from little rest and the strain of events I couldn't fathom, I lay on the hay near my wife and fell into dreamless sleep...

It was several days later, as I recall it, that a trio of richly dressed astrologer-philosophers, commonly known as Magi, appeared at the door of the small room the innkeeper had found for us the day following the birth. For weeks, they told us, they had been on their way from somewhere far east of the Jordan; they spoke of a star, as astrologers well may. The truly surprising thing, though, was that they brought gifts, costly gifts that had been prepared for a kingly birth. Less surprising to me was their kneeling beside my son's manger-cradle.

Thus the story I've had to tell... As I promised at the beginning of what must seem a very strange narrative, I've shared with you as simply as I can all that occurred during my oldest son's coming into the world.

If my strength holds, there is much more that I must write before it is too late. I must tell something of the years that have lain between and the growing evidences these years have brought that my son is peculiarly imbued with the spirit and the power of a loving God. Our Jesus is not the Messiah that most people have expected, and this is why I fear so. Through the years of my son's youth I have grown to understand what Messiahship may really mean: that it is selflessness, forgiveness, costly love, a sense of serving others that is particularly joyful, and an abandonment of one's self that makes other folk better than they are, sometimes better than at first they want to be, but which once understood makes them aspire and reach upward.

This is Messiahship that reflects the reality of a loving God. This is my son. I have shared with you all that I recall of his birth... I wonder whether you will hear of him again, and that if you do, whether you will understand...

Chapter 4

The Innkeeper

Note: The translation of the following document, produced as far as is known in the first century A.D., has been difficult both physically — because of the ravages of time — and linguistically. Aramaic is a form of Syriac, which in turn has both Greek and Hebrew elements in it, two languages which are far removed from one another in linguistic laws. The writer knew all too well how to use the language of his day and place; he is idiomatic almost to a fault. Accomplished modern scholars of first-century Judean Aramaic are not infrequently puzzled by him.

The present translation, however, is generally considered to be remarkably true to the sense of the original. Modern verb forms, especially, are substituted wherever these are deemed best to convey the writer's intent.

Perhaps I am writing what no one will ever read. He is gone — and there seem now to be so few who really cared. In these two years that have elapsed since my return to home and profession, I have tried to think and to recall with some clarity. I should add in honesty that since the spell of his presence has been taken away, I have half expected that, like awakening from a dream, I would throw off the past, throw off what he would call his "yoke," and find myself free once more.

Curiously, though, I haven't cared to be free. The memory of what he was — and perhaps something more — seem of far greater importance than the freedom and forgetfulness that now could be mine. I have come to realize that alive or dead he continues to be my Master and my Lord. Alive or dead, I continue his slave; nothing else now seems possible... It was less than a year ago in a Jerusalem synagogue that I heard Peter remark publicly that he was convinced that Jesus was continuing on, exercising that strange, compelling, intimate power upon those who had been close to him in this life. I have to agree.

"In this life..." It is a strange phrase for me to use, you will say, particularly those of you who knew me earlier, before he came along — knew me simply as the Innkeeper of Bethlehem, one who was foolish enough one day to follow off in the train of a wandering teacher whom more than one wise man labeled a fool. One might gather that in very truth I believe that there is a life beyond this one.

Let me say clearly that I do so believe. I believe because he believed... If this reasoning seems circuitous, I can only answer that when you joined him with sincere intent, even if only for a limited while, it became impossible not to believe in that which for him was a matter of trust.

I remember one of the temple authorities once remarking in our hearing that Jesus spoke with authority. He did indeed: he spoke with a strangely compelling authority which I now believe came from beyond himself. Clearly this was because Jesus was a channel — a channel much more than an initiator; he gave himself utterly and without restraint to be God's most sensitive and responsive communication point among men. As he so often said himself, his power to heal the sick, to still the sea, to work what we call miracles, was not his own; it was simply the infinite power of God flowing through him. This is why those of us who knew him best could only describe him as God in human flesh, or God among us, or sometimes as he himself would suggest, God's only Son. All of these were our poor attempts to describe in words our indescribable experience of him.

For a reason which I am about to relate, the Master's hold on me went back much farther in time than it did with others of his band; they merely saw me as the elder brother of the group. I was a generation older than any of them; he knew why, because one day when I had become sure of my facts, I told him.

Even at the time, I understood why the others mistrusted me. First, I am of the house of David, of the pure lineage of Judah; second, I am a landowner. Finally, most serious guilt of all, I can read and write. All of these things set me unavoidably apart from the simple men and women who made up much of the Master's following. He himself had the quality of accepting each of us for what he or she honestly was as a person. He knew that I was one of his...

None of those who have been with Jesus in these latter years, with the exception of his mother, knew of the circumstances surrounding his birth. Matthew has spoken of his intent to write a biography of him, and I am told that young John Mark is taking notes from Peter's street-preaching which he intends to use as the basis for a history of the Master's life,

Neither of these, though, knew of the things that surrounded the Master's genesis, his beginning. It is my concern that these oddly inspiring circumstances shall not sink into oblivion; it is this that leads me to write the following pages. The tragedy for me has always been that in a sense I was not a participant, at least to the extent I have later wished. At the time, mine rather was a supporting role: I write as an observer.

History's verdict may be that what I shall write betrays only my own lively imagination. Let me say here that as you read, you will find much of it well-nigh incredible. As I think back, there are ways in which I myself fight with a sense of the incredible, even now.

Admitting all of this, I yet must write... I must record the events of those strange and memorable weeks.

Let me add a further word simply as a matter of personal identity... Those who have occasion to stay frequently here in our Inn of Chimham will be familiar with its honored history. Our family has been proud of the fact that because of the kindness of our forefather Barzilai to David, then a young exile, the later King David bestowed upon Barzilai and his son Chimham certain tracts of land here in the Bethlehem region. A small portion of the walls in the present structure remain from the original inn built centuries ago by Chimham himself; I have been put to no little expense lately to preserve them...

Of importance, too, is the fact that our family has retained ownership of the Inn through unbroken lines of descent from David's day to our own. Chimham is known from Dan to Beersheba, not for size or elegance but simply as an honored symbol of the history of Yahweh's people. The Inn's keepers down the centuries have been men of civic and religious responsibility and, for their times, men of culture.

* * *

It was in the year of the Roman census which Augustus had ordered to be conducted in the Hebrew manner — as altered in certain practicalities by the Romans themselves. Some of you will recall it; this was in the second year before the death of Herod the Idumean. I might add that here in Bethlehem this Herod is remembered for only one thing — a brutal massacre of infants up to the age of two years. The matter was hushed up in Jerusalem; it could not be hushed up here.

The first link in the curious chain of circumstances which I relate to you was the proclamation of this census. I recognized immediately that if it indeed were to be done in the Hebrew style, all of those who had even the remotest connection with the Bethlehem branch of the house of David would converge upon us. So, in fact, it was; as early as two days before the proclaimed date every one of our modest supply of rooms was full and many folk were accepting pallets in the hallways.

As I recall, it was on the last night before the census was to commence that a young couple, weary from travel and strain, showed themselves at the door. They were simply-dressed peasants, and the woman, slumped wearily on their riding animal, was about to have a child. The young man in low tones explained their predicament.

I had been turning people away for almost two days, but here was a case where something had to be done. I thought quickly. The only place of shelter I could offer was our rear stable, which really was not as crude as it may sound. I should explain that our stables run back, cave-like, into the hill against which the Inn of Chimham stands. Periodically across the years successive innkeepers have added to these. The most remote stable we rarely use simply because of its inaccessibility... I suggested this possibility to the young man; he looked once at his weary wife, took a long breath and accepted.

I sent the boy to clear any animals from the far inner stable and dispatched a room-girl for blankets; the young couple had very few. Then I took my cloak and escorted them personally to the appointed place. It was a slow trip; the young woman's time was coming fast upon her and the young man carried her in his arms the latter half of the way. We found some fresh hay and a clean saddle-blanket for her to lie on and I saw to it that she was made as comfortable as possible under the circumstances. Only thirty-one at the time, I suddenly felt inward panic at what might next happen; I was fortunately relieved and invited out of the room with the bustling arrival of my beloved and efficient Tabitha with three women and a host of blankets in tow. I hurried back to the common room and my guests and gave little further thought to the remote inward stable.

It was early in the morning, in the first hours after midnight, when I was awakened by the boy. He reported that three shepherds, of all people, had demanded entrance into the stable to see the new baby that had been born; one of them, he said, had mumbled something about a "king."

The shepherds in our nearby fields are generally a sober and respected group; the flocks they tend are destined for sacrificial use, and most of these men regard their work as a holy calling... I was immediately awake and alert. Why this excitement over a new baby — and at this uncivilized hour in the morning? I arose from my pallet, took my robe, and hurried toward the stables. Seeing one of my two room-girls standing at the opening into the innermost enclosure, I paused — but she beckoned me inside.

The peasant family looked normal enough. Someone had thought of using an empty manger for a cradle, and inside of this, lying on some clean hay, was the new baby, carefully wrapped in one of Tabitha's blankets and, of course, deep in sleep. The mother was resting nearby and the father was standing at her feet. Both of them were watching the shepherds — the father nervously alert, the young mother quite relaxed.

Inexplicably and quite surprisingly, the shepherds were kneeling, of all things, around the manger: strange conduct indeed... As I stared at them in silence, I noted on the faces of the two whom I could see an expression of amazement and a sort of tenderness and — I can only call it what it was — reverence, as they gazed at the sleeping child.

As I stood and surveyed all of this I began to feel embarrassed — left out of the situation; there was something uncanny here. To relieve my discomfiture I turned to go, mumbling to one of the shepherds to see me before they returned to the fields.

All three came to me later, where I stood in wait at the outer courtyard gate. It was cold but they were dressed lightly; they told me that they had made their way up from the fields so exhilarated that they hadn't felt the cold.

The eldest of them, Alpheus by name, explained what had happened. I had known the shepherd since my childhood, when he would often let me sit with him on an outlook while he spun an engrossing story for me. The story he was telling me now, however, sounded more of a made-up tale than any he had told me in earlier years. You will not be disposed to believe it as you read; I had difficulty in believing any of it — then...

Alpheus said that as his group had been watching their flocks out on the meadow, suddenly they had been conscious of a presence; that is the way he put it — conscious of a presence. He claimed that they had been *told* about the birth of the baby and — notice this — that they would find him in a manger. Finally, it had seemed to them that they heard music in the air and all about them.

Alpheus saw the doubt in my eyes, and he understood. As though he felt the uselessness of further words, he turned on his heel and disappeared into the night; the others followed him.

I returned to my pallet and found myself lying awake, thinking. I couldn't dismiss out of hand the sincerity in his eyes and voice as Alpheus had talked to me, and I couldn't dismiss the reverence that had been in the faces and bodies of the others as I had seen them beside the manger. But — voices in the air? No — I concluded that surely there must be a sensible explanation and finally I slept.

Within the week I moved the peasant family indoors as soon as I was able. It would surely be some days before the woman would feel able to travel.

Several nights later, well into darkness, the peasant family again had visitors. These were stranger by far than the shepherds. A retinue appeared at the head of the street — mules, servants and all, following three large and lavishly adorned camels. These were clearly travellers of means and importance.

Rather flustered, I must admit, I met them at the courtyard entry; they were swarthy Magi — astrologer-princes — from the far eastern deserts; to my eye they were over-dressed and bejeweled.

Speaking from the height of his palanquin, which was somehow braced against the hump in the back of his oddly shaped beast, the man in the lead addressed me in halting Aramaic, politely but in the attitude of one who wears authority about him.

"Where is the young king who is to have been born here?"

For several embarrassing moments I looked blankly up at him, making no sense of his question. Then, with a chill curling up my back, I recalled with shocking recognition the shepherds and the message they had been given in the night. Here was a second word of a "king"...

"He — if you'll come with me, I'll take you to the baby that was born in one of our stables. I — I'm not sure —" My voice trailed off as I was suddenly afraid of saying too much, claiming too much. I had heard a little about eastern Magi; they studied the stars in order to chart the future, were held in much esteem within their own cultures, and usually belonged to the higher social classes.

For the first time in this whole strange adventure, I was suddenly close to panic. Shepherds, with their word of music in the air and a voice speaking to them of a king, and now this...these strangers...these aristocrats from the east, asking about a newly born king... The already confused pattern was becoming terrifying.

The three visitors in their pointed shoes and betassled robes came toward me, and I turned to lead them. They followed me silently, with a pair of their servants bringing up the rear. I led them down the short hall, tapped gently on the doorsill of the room occupied by the young family, pulled aside the curtain over the doorway and stepped aside.

I had intended to retreat back to the reception chamber as a worthy innkeeper is expected to do, but I looked once before turning away, and I was lost. I remained in the room, against a wall.

You who read will find it difficult to credit what I now have to relate. I shall state with the simple truth all that I can recall of the next minutes.

In the humble setting of that room, the three aristocrats from afar first looked at each other, then at the young mother who was gazing back at them with genuine amazement but yet with quiet welcome. The young father moved over to the simple cradle we had improvised, very clearly to be on guard; there was anything but welcome in his expression.

Silence reigned for a full minute as the visitors came to terms with the room, the parents and my presence. Then they moved together the three or four steps across the room to the cradle and stood looking down into it. A yet longer silence ensued. Twice they looked at each other, as if exchanging a wordless question or a message, and then down again.

Finally one of them turned to the others. I recognized the one who had addressed me from atop his beast; he spoke in that still halting Aramaic, no doubt out of courtesy to the young couple. He spoke slowly and from out of deep thought.

"I feel that our journey has ended," he said. "It is not as we expected..." He paused. Then, looking long again at the sleeping child and speaking quietly but more strongly, "I feel that this is he for whom we have searched. The star was not a lie, Ormuzd be praised!"

The speaker then turned to the cradle and slowly knelt on the dusty floor of the little chamber. The others in their turn did likewise. There was silence again, during which I noticed that all three were in prayer. No one in the room moved. I looked once at the young parents. The young man's near hostility had turned to a very simple and ill-concealed amazement; the mother, resting easily on her pallet, caught and held my attention. She was looking on with warm interest but — notice this particularly — with little surprise. Once she caught my eye and smiled briefly. As I stood against the wall in the silence, I thought again of shepherds who also had knelt in the presence of this tiny new child.

My reverie was interrupted by one of the kneeling visitors who, without rising to his feet, turned toward the doorway and nodded; I had forgotten the two servants, whom I now heard stepping quickly down the hall. They returned laden with gifts, in the manner of their country — splendid gifts planned for a young prince. The Magi rose and presented these with easy formality to the young couple, speaking quietly to each other and to them as they did so.

It was in that moment, I believe, that somehow the words and movements of the visitors came together in my mind; with sudden clarity, I recognized what was happening: these wise-men from across the eastern deserts had come in search of a newborn king, and here in my inn they believed that they had found him...

Soon after this presentation of gifts, the visitors retreated from the room. They remained for a night on the edge of town; their servants set up an encampment there that was more splendid by far than the finest of rooms I could have offered them. In the morning they were gone; we didn't see them again.

I had never in my life before been so inwardly wracked with emotional and mental turmoil. On the second morning I was driven by sleeplessness and inner tension to the young couple themselves. I don't know what I had expected, but I was greeted with quiet hospitality when I begged entrance to their chamber. The gifts of the Magi were arranged along one wall, a display ill-fitted to its surroundings. The young mother was sitting comfortably on a blanket-covered bench now; it was clear that the little family would not be long with us in the Inn.

There were sincere words of thanks for my kindness to them in their first extremity and in the various visitations that had followed. The child was resting easily, awake in his cradle. I took courage...

Beginning with some of the ordinary questions about who really we were dealing with in this young couple, I discovered some personal facts very quickly: they were not long married, they were from the hill village of Nazareth in the Galilee, and he was a carpenter. Gradually I brought the conversation around to their child; very shortly, and to my own surprise, I found myself sharing some of my innermost turmoil, the troubled fruit of the recent past days.

"Your son," I said. "The child..." And then in a sort of agony I couldn't hide, "Tell me what — no, *who* he is!"

After a brief silence, it was the young mother who spoke. "I — I believe I can tell you," she said. "You see, Joseph and I believe that our child has a strange and high destiny." Then, embarrassed, "Of course, I suppose many young parents hold such a hope for their child."

It was the young father's turn. "No, Mary; that's not enough." He turned to me. "You've seen some of the surprising and upsetting things — the visitors we've had. What do you make of them?"

I had no answer. Into the silence, the young mother spoke.

"Joseph and I, each of us, have our own reasons for holding to high — and frightening — expectations. Joseph believes —" here she paused and looked me directly in the eyes — "Joseph believes our child may well become the Messiah, the one who somehow is to save his people."

Again, she paused. Then, "You have seen," she said, "that Joseph is not alone in this hope — no, this expectation... The shepherds who came to visit us —"

"I know about that," I interrupted. "They told me." My voice was harsher than I intended. I was under an emotional strain the like of which I had never before endured. "They told me that they heard voices in the night..."

"Yes," she said. There was a pause.

I spoke again. "What of these others — these Magi?"

She looked at me. "The wise-men followed a star, so they told us." She spoke with a simplicity that rose serenely above argument or denial. "I've never heard of anyone following a star... I'm — I'm not quite sure what they meant. They said that the star seemed to stop right over Bethlehem... Of course," and here she spoke quickly, out of her own thoughts, "Of course, a star seems to move if *you* move..."

Again there was a pause. The young man's eyes never left her face. It was as though he was living through with her the words she was speaking and the memory they evoked.

Then, deeply thoughtful, "Whatever the visits we've had may mean," she said, "this I believe: I believe that God led both the shepherds so close at hand and the travellers from so far away, and that he brought them to this place, to — to my child..."

It wasn't long thereafter that the prescribed forty days had elapsed, and the young couple with their son went to our local synagogue for the purification ceremonies. They returned to their room at the Inn for only a day or two, as it happened. They left early on the second night quite suddenly. Joseph, the young father, said something to the effect that their lives were in danger, or that the child's life was in danger; at the time, I didn't understand him. They departed quickly southward, toward Gaza, promising to return if God opened the way.

I didn't understand then. I did, two days later, when the soldiers arrived in town without warning and killed a few of our children — on Herod's orders. As I say, the matter was hushed up in Jerusalem. The soldiers themselves had no stomach for the task, and they affected not to see many of the youngsters. They had been given their orders, though, on pain of death if they failed. It was — it was not pleasant.

I asked one of them the reason for the shameful act, and I was given an honest and bitter answer... It seemed that Herod had heard of the birth — yes, the birth of a king — and he sought to eliminate this threat to his throne and its succession.

I didn't see the peasant family again. I didn't hear a word, not again, until almost a year later as I recall; a trader with several camels coming from the north put a small parchment into my hand. It simply read in rather cribbed hand-script, "We are safe here in the north. Thank you for your concern."

Some things one doesn't really forget. Certain events in our lives seem never to slip away into the past; they are eternally present with us. My own experience with this has helped me to understand in these recent years what the Master meant when he spoke, as so often he did, of eternal life.

I can speak of this now because more than a quarter of a century after the events I have here related, I saw him again. I was travelling in the north, and I came upon him speaking to a group of people in a large field not far from Tiberias. It was a curiously diverse group, drawn from all levels of our society. I can only say that all through the years between I had somehow been waiting for him; having heard that a travelling teacher here in the north was drawing many people to his message, I suppose that without realizing it I was watching for him. Will you believe me when I say that I knew who he was even before I was yet close enough to hear his voice?

It isn't strange that in view of all of these things, I became one of his own. I came to realize, as time went on and as my experience of him went on, that even if without intention, I had given myself to him back down the years when he lay, a new-born child, under my roof.

Others will write of his ministry, of his command over the inner dimensions of one's life, of his glorious victory even in death. But I — I have wanted to write of his birth: this because it was then that the seed was planted that finally led me, through all of my doubting and questions, to know that through life and death and beyond, he is and ever shall be the Lord of all — of all people — and their Saviour.

Perhaps some of you who shall read these pages will find a key to faith and hope and trust — faith in him and hope because of him and so, trust forevermore in God and his presence with us — you may find that key as I did in the story of his coming into the world.

I have given it to you simply as I lived it. More I cannot do, but surely in the power of his abiding spirit, I have done enough.

Chapter 5

Behold, Wise Men From The East Came

Wise men came from the East...

I'd occasionally wondered about those Wise Men and their strange journey — so much a part of our Christmas tradition, and yet so little understood.

Then — one day, a lot of things suddenly broke into clarity. It wasn't really that my hoped-for doctorate at Princeton University quickly moved several notches closer, nor was it simply that the summer heat of Jerusalem was unexpectedly made almost pleasant by several days of delightful breezes playing about its 2,600 foot elevation.

The experience, in fact, was solidly scholarly but intensely centered in the personal dimension. It was as though my usual experience of Christmas, dependably secular despite the several Holy Land Christmases I'd lived through, had suddenly been blessed with the gift of life...

The details needn't long detain us: I had been at work on a file of unattached first century manuscripts. There was one of several sheets that with gloved hands and considerable care I began to unfold. Covered with a fine dust were the pages of a rather rough vellum. Translation proved to be a slow process; I'm not as comfortable in ancient Persian dialects as I am in Old Hebrew. I struggled at first. As I warmed to the task, though, it became clear that it was a personal letter with which I was working.

The writer was apparently a Zoroastrian priest. If you're unacquainted with the Zoroastrians, it will help to note that Zoroaster was a Persian prophet whose birth is shrouded in antiquity and myth, but whose wisdom and spirituality were very real. His followers were and are monotheists; they worship one God, the creator of all the earth. Their name for him is Ahura Mazda, or "Lord All Knowing." Usually they shorten this Ahura Mazda to the simpler "Ormuzd." The Parsis in India carry on the teachings and faith of Zoroaster today.

It became clear as I worked that the ancient writer of the letter was addressing a brother priest whose friendship was a very dear thing to him and of long standing. As Magi, or Wise Men, skilled in ancient astrology and omens, these two were of considerable position and means, no doubt demanding and receiving the respect due their station in life.

Perhaps all of this is enough by way of preliminary explanation. My occasional use of modern English idiom in the task of translation is simply in the name of getting on with the job. On the other hand, you will also understand that where my linguistic seems stiff or formal or even archaic, one sometimes avoids this in dealing with an ancient text only at the peril of doing serious injustice to the original... The letter opens without salutation, possibly due to manuscript damage.

* * *

It is not easy, my Tansar, for me to bring you to understand all that has happened since I embarked on my fateful trip to the west. Especially is it difficult for me to break off a relationship which has been as completely pleasant and as congenial as has that between you and myself. And yet I must do so. You know as well as I the demanding and exclusive nature of the faith we have shared; certainly it is not a system to be trifled with. The great Prophet made *that*, at least, abundantly clear. Who would follow Zoroaster may follow none other.

Tansar, I ask you to prepare yourself for what I must now say: I fear that I myself, who have always been in the forefront of those who would cry out against heretics — I fear that now *I* am bordering upon such a way of life and thought.

It will no doubt be long before I can completely understand all that has happened. But this I know: *It is no longer possible for me to continue on as a teacher and priest in the footsteps of the Prophet.*

I had been for so long contented and filled with an abiding inner satisfaction. *You* know, you who were in the training for such a length of years with me. There were none who took more relish than I in memorizing passages from the *Avesta* — both the books of law, and the songs of our faith. Together we were ordained into the priesthood, you and I; together we have travelled the years. Together we have followed the stars in their courses, both the fixed star Yazatas and the planets, those special heavenly creations of our father Ormuzd. Together so long, and now no longer — for Tansar, I am sinking into the sloughs of what will seem to you to be heresy.

I know you, Friend, and I know you wonder at my inability to pull myself from this internal discord to pick up again the peaceful and systematic strands of normal life — strands which now for me are so tangled... I need to say to you that no more compelling were the seven visions of our great Prophet than has been the experience of these past months for me. Surely you know me well enough to realize that only an incident of deep personal significance could lead me to the renunciation I now must make.

Yes — I must resign from our brotherhood, Tansar, and I must leave you — you who have been brother and companion to me in deepest degree. And — I must go in search...

This is surely a strange thing to say, but believe me when I tell you that it is even a stranger thing to feel: this because I know not for what I search. I only know that a force has been let loose upon the earth...but let me begin at the beginning. Certainly the fullest possible explanation is due you to whom I owe so much.

The story begins on that evening which I know you must remember as clearly as I, in the late fall. There had been rain for three days previously, and now that the rain had ceased the air was unusually transparent; the leagues of distance across our Parthian plains seemed within the range of a single stone's throw. It was a night for walking and for dreaming, if one were inclined; you will recall how our townspeople were out on the streets enjoying the change of weather, dark as the night was. It seemed that all of Arsacia was determined to spend the night afoot.

You and I had betaken ourselves to that particular hillock from which so often we had made our calculations on the movement of the planets. You will recall that we had noted earlier, on a clear night before the rain had come, that Saturn and Jupiter had taken up queer positions; quite contrary to their usual placement, they were conjoined within the zodiacal sign of Pisces. You noticed it first, and I dryly remarked upon the wine we had enjoyed at dinner — and then I saw it too.

For days afterward we talked about it, struggled in argument, came to no conclusion. Then upon this lovely night following the rain, it was I who made the new discovery. Mars had joined the other two planets.

I remember how I rubbed my eyes before I said anything to you. Were the heavens going to pieces before us? Then I looked again and pointed it out to you. We could hardly contain ourselves, I recall, as we returned to our charts in the temple to verify our discovery. And — we found that we were correct: Mars did not belong where we now observed it to be.

The next few nights, you will remember, we were out on the hill together. I wonder if it was a touch of the prophetic that was upon us those evenings. Do you recall how our conversation turned always toward a strange conception that has been rife throughout the world, even to Babylon and the western sea? It is the conviction that a new and powerful monarch is to arise somewhere off to the west. Do you remember how we discussed it, struggled over it and wondered? It was purely idle speculation with us at first, I suppose.

What I was too sensitive to tell you, Tansar — and I have since cursed myself for my cowardice — what I didn't tell you is that I slept little during those nights after we had returned to our pallets. The reason for my unrest should not surprise you, though doubtless you will thrust it away from you: surely you are aware that the coming of a king has always been announced, to those who have eyes to see, by a significant movement in the heavens...

I am aware, Tansar, that you brand all of this as mere superstition. It can't be said of every king within our own history, I grant willingly enough; perhaps it can be *proved* of none of them. Such has always been your contention.

Night after restless night, though, deep within myself I couldn't shake the feeling that Ormuzd, be his name praised, was striving to speak to me... Bear with me, beloved Friend; I can do no other than share with you the truth of what I experienced. I felt that a message was seeking to break through to me — and yet, not simply to me. It was as if reality, living truth, lay waiting to be opened to all people, if only some would discover it.

If only some would discover it... Perhaps this thought was in my mind that last evening on which we journeyed to our observation hill together. I need not detail for you what happened there; you will remember it well enough. If it was painful for you, know that it was doubly so for me, in light of the tension under which I so strangely found myself.

...You will still maintain that the star was not there. I know now, beyond all shadow of doubt, that it *was* there... I have returned home, across these weary weeks of mountain and desert, to see you and tell you, and now, at home in my beloved Arsacia, I have decided to leave again with the rising of the sun — without seeing you. During these long night hours it comes to me that it is not yet time to share with you all that has happened; hence this written word. I am dispatching it by young Amir; he will place it in your hand within the very hour of my departure. It has come to me this night *that the star was there only for those who were prepared to see it.* I can make no further explanation to you that would make sense, as yet. Someday, perhaps. Ahead of me lies a quest, perhaps a long one. I may return one day, certain of my message to you.

Think back, Tansar. You will remember how we stood there upon the hillside and that I clutched your arm. Right between Saturn and Mars it was, Friend... Oh, I know. As you read this you are shaking your head... Or am I wrong? Did it later grow brighter for you, too, so that its presence was beyond any doubting? I shall never know, shall I — until I return to you with my pilgrimage completed.

It was very tiny, I admit. With all of your wisdom and experience, your eyes were never as strong as mine. Placement of the smaller stars on our charts was always my task; quite simply, you couldn't see them in the heavens. On this particular night, I could see the star only by looking a bit to one side and marking it out of the corner of my eye. But it *was there*, Tansar. It was a new star where there had been only blackness before.

You argued with me, I remember. The conjoining of Saturn and Jupiter was almost too much to believe, and then when Mars joined them — well, here was a genuine strain on your sense of the credible. These things, however, you saw for yourself; their reality was undeniable. This *new* star: no, this was too much for one season. You refused to believe what my own eyes told me. I argued and pled with you, all to no avail.

I suppose those nights awake upon my pallet had much to do with it. I couldn't shake my strange sense of imminent upheaval. Disaster or triumph, life or death — I couldn't guess what it was to be, but despite all, I couldn't shake the feeling. I suppose I was tense and a bit weary, and you laughed at me a little, Tansar. But I saw the star; it was there and — you wouldn't listen.

This much of my story you know. What follows will be new to you. It may make very little intelligible sense to you, but I'm unrepentant. I shall relate only what happened, with as little comment as possible. Perhaps some day you will be grasped by it as I have been.

Grasped by what, you're asking now? My answer: I know very little, yet. But I do know that it is real and compelling. If I see you again in this life, I shall be able to tell you.

It was late at night, a scant three hours before dawn, that I prepared to leave. I had awakened only Khorda, my personal servant. I desired no retinue, but he insisted upon coming with me himself, and I allowed him. He has been with me since.

As we left the sleeping city behind us and set off south-westward on the road to Babylon, the strange star was brighter... I can see in my mind's eye the doubt written on your face, but the star *was* clearer. It grew in brightness steadily during the next few nights. It was on the fourth night that Khorda himself saw it, and verified what I was beginning to see as an almost unnatural and therefore scarcely believable brightness.

I am not entirely sure what impelled me westward. Playing its part was the very thing that you are so inclined to ridicule — the common conviction among many for the last three generations that a king is to arise to the west. The new star seemed to me so evident a message of some momentous event.

We travelled alone, Khorda and I, for several days — a foolish thing to do, I know; I can imagine your frown of disapproval as you read this. But no man bothered us.

Then it was that a strange thing occurred. We had stopped for the midday meal in a small hamlet on the slopes of the first hills to which the traveller comes before dropping down into the valley of the River Copratas. Another seer was there in the inn commonroom and we fell into conversation. He was a quiet man, much my elder; an extensive retinue was in the courtyard but he was dining alone. When I discovered that he was bound for the capital of Judea, my interest quickened. It was not many moments before we discovered that ours was a common quest. His home was Carmana, not far from the great Carmanian Desert. He had seen the star, my Tansar, just as had I, and he told me without embarrassment that he was going to find a king, the king who would some day conquer the evil forces of Ahriman and the world of darkness and that would make straight the way for our Lord and Father Ormuzd... I had to recognize that he had thought more deeply on his quest than had I, and that his journey was clearer in its intent and direction.

In the morning, we travelled on together. His retinue provided a comfortable protection as we descended into the rich river plains that must be crossed before one reaches the great city of Babylon. It was there one night that we came upon a small encampment by the river, and the two of us became three.

He was a man of wisdom and astrology from Persepolis, and — yes, Tansar, he too had seen the star. Very young he was, and his retinue, though small, spoke of considerable wealth. We stayed the night together and departed upon our way together in the coolness of the dawn.

I remember well that evening as we lay for some time on the river bank before going to our tents. The star was becoming brighter with each passing night. One could look directly at it now without locating Mars first. Ours was a rich fellowship as we shared our dream and our hope.

As we travelled the succeeding weeks together ever westward, that dream became a trust and a faith for all three of us. Something lay beyond that ever-receding sunset. It was not for nothing that our Father Ormuzd had led us toward each other.

We discovered a strange congeniality. Despite our widely separated abodes, we were knit together by several common convictions. For one, we knew that there was far more suffering upon the earth than was our Father's will. You know well, Tansar, how often I have shared with you my conviction that our common people must be more fully provided for, that the laws of our land must permit a fuller sharing, even at the cost of a bit less luxury for such as you and me.

How we argued then, the two of us, about illness. I felt then as I do now that suffering is not the will of Ormuzd — that sickness is not sent as punishment, and that love rules the universe. How you laughed at me in your good-natured way at that one...

Tansar, these men had thought and dreamed as I have thought and dreamed. I no longer felt emotionally strained and alone and outcast, as so often even with you I have felt. Here was a measure of completion, and I think it was felt by the other two as by me; they, too, had been lonely in their dream. Now we shared each other's dream, for together we looked for the same kind of a better world than this...

The weather was growing cooler during the last days of our journey, and rain was falling lightly on the late afternoon that we came within sight of the holy city of the Judeans. Jerusalem is interesting, Tansar — beautiful from afar as the road climbs over the hill called Olivet, but ugly and a bit odorous when one is within the walls. Also, it is too full of people and too interlaced with Roman soldiers. This is natural, since Rome is much more enamored of this crowded little corridor colony than of our far-off desert reaches.

The crowds in the streets made way for our caravan and watched respectfully as we rode by. I was much more interested in the squalor of their living conditions than in their respect, however. Desperately they needed someone to raise their vision above the level of mere food and sleep. The people I saw had fallen far below the high hopes of their prophetic writers. They seemed to be merely grubbing through life, so intent on the material that they missed completely that which we have been taught is eternal.

I suppose, in fact, that they were like so many people everywhere, the masses I saw in Babylon and in the farms beyond it, the fishermen on the rivers, the tradesmen from the far Indies... people missing the whole point and meaning of life...

Ruminating on this as we entered the city, we headed for the most likely place for the birth of a new royal child — the palace of the King of Judea, one "Herod" by name. He is only partly a king, of course; Rome really rules the land, but it allows him to preserve certain appearances. In his way, he does exercise considerable brute force.

The situation actually fits him. When we were shown into his presence, it was immediately evident that he is little more than a brutal charlatan. Beneath his rich clothing he was obviously shallow, sensuous, self-centered.

His courtiers were respectful of us and bowed themselves out after showing us to his audience room. I wasted no time on any but the barest formalities and asked him abruptly if a new child had been born in his household. I added, of course, that we had seen what we believed to be the star signalling the birth of such a future king.

Herod was visibly shaken at all of this and replied in the negative. Then he asked us to tarry while he made further inquiries. In less than ten minutes he had surrounded himself with several of his advisers; present also were some who apparently ruled the temple in the city. Herod inquired of this motley crew where the great king, the "Meshia" as he called such a one, was supposed to be born. There was no hesitation about the answer that these worthies gave him: Bethlehem, they said, was the city spoken of by their prophetic writers. This later proved to be a rather small town about two leagues along the gentle ridge to the south of Jerusalem...

It is surprising as I look back upon it, Tansar, how natural it all seemed. One would have thought that we should have been beset by doubts at this point; why should *we* be singled out to witness the coming into time of the great leader for whom these Hebrews had been waiting over the centuries? It couldn't be; surely we had been mistaken.

This, perhaps, is what we ought to have been thinking — but it was not. I remember having the fleeting thought once again that the star had been there for all people to see, but the only ones who did see it were those ready for it — those with eyes to see.

It was at this point that Herod, half doubting and half worried that we had stumbled onto truth, suggested that we try Bethlehem. As we paused in the doorway of his audience room for a final farewell, he called out with unmistakable sarcasm that if we found the Meshia we should let him know, so that he could come and pay homage also... I doubt that any one of us would have troubled to set foot in his palace again.

The trip to Bethlehem seemed best postponed until the following day. We stayed the night at a modest inn just outside the walls on the Bethlehem road. It was a clear, cold night, I remember; the rain had ceased, leaving an unusual clarity in the air. I recall how, as sleep tarried, I seemed to sense a tension in the atmosphere; it was as if all nature were waiting and watching, though this may have been only a reflection of my own inner wondering and — yes — my anticipation.

I heard later in the common gossip that at sometime during the preceding days, shepherds on the eastern slopes not far out of the town were visited by what they spoke of as a divine message of some sort, telling them of the birth of a king. I was unable to locate any of these men to verify the rumor...

After a brief ride the next morning we entered Bethlehem and found it in a practical uproar because of a census that was being conducted; for some reason which made sense to the Roman authorities but hardly to anyone else, citizens from all over the land, in order to be counted, had to report to the city or town which had historically been the seat of their tribal lineage. So it was that the grubby hamlet was full to the bursting point with outsiders from all over Palestine. It was obvious immediately that few of these strangers would have the slightest interest in the birth of a royal child. Their concern was limited to where they could spend the night and where they could obtain a meal.

I sent Khorda to ask questions on the little main street, and he returned swiftly with word that confirmed the birth of a child a few days before; minor local attention had been called to it because the birth had concerned some outsiders, a young couple coming from the north for the census. The innkeeper, to whom we now went for information, revealed that the child had been born in his stables, of all places, behind the village inn.

We turned away in disappointment. This stable business couldn't have anything to do with our quest in search of a royal birth. An hour passed as we continued our questioning, with fading hope, of any who might be able to help. It had become clear that as far as any of the townspeople knew, this birth at the inn involved the only child born recently in the hamlet, or liable to be. More to put the final ending to our Bethlehem search than for any other reason, we reluctantly returned to the inn.

The innkeeper replied modestly to our question; a day after the birth one of his rooms had become available amidst the general confusion reigning in the town, and he had moved the grateful young couple into it with their new child. He led us to an open doorway and moved aside the curtain for us to enter.

As I wrote at the beginning of this long letter, Tansar, I can only set down here what truly happened. Though your credulity may be taxed, my friend, please bear with me to the end.

How can I explain it? With what gifted and convincing words can I relate how *here I knew that our pilgrimage had come to its end*? What are those memorable moments that come now and again into one's life — brief experiences of sheer and brilliantly clear insight when truth is suddenly and surely there, and one knows this beyond all doubting? I suppose it is in such moments that one reaches out and touches eternity. One doesn't analyze too much; one merely gives himself over to a kind of quiet joy, knowing fully that here is complete blessing and reality — this minute in time.

Such a moment happened in my life as we entered the room where the man and his wife and the child were. There seemed nothing out of the ordinary in what we saw, except that the infant was lying in a small manger filled with fresh hay in lieu of a cradle; they had moved this in from the stable, nothing more suitable being at hand. The child was asleep and looked very tiny and very new. The mother was quite young, dressed in the simple peasant garb seen everywhere in these small Hebrew towns; the father was also young, and stood a bit self-consciously by his wife as we came near, as though to protect her. I suppose we did seem a bit formidable, and certainly over-dressed, in that simple place.

I had forgotten, Tansar, how strange we must have looked to them, entering as we did quite unannounced. In fact, I had forgotten even the common civility of stating my name — because as I looked at the sleeping child, the strange feeling of unexplained joy I've tried to describe to you came over me.... Tansar, I dropped to my knees — *I* — on the worn stones of that simple floor.

Several moments passed before I realized that my companions had been similarly affected, though they were still standing a little behind me. We had each brought gifts with us, though we had expected to offer them amidst kingly trappings; we were reduced to sending a servant scurrying back to the camels to fetch them... I suppose it was an incongruous scene, but — this, too, was strange — it didn't *seem* incongruous. It was absolutely authentic, and as I look back upon it, it still seems authentic beyond any doubting...

Tansar, to my last day in this life, I shall believe that I was then in the presence of the most kingly creature ever to wear earth about him. Don't require explanations of me: I don't have them. But I must tell you that I am staking my future — all that I am and all that I have — on the conviction that came over me and the moment of stark beauty and utter reality that I experienced when I stepped into that royal presence.

There is little more to tell you, Friend. I have realized during these long night hours that I can never bring all of this alive for you — not now — and so I've labored to express on the parchment what I cannot yet bring to you in person. The child we visited that morning will come to his adulthood one day. I must know what it all means; I must know what his kingdom is to be, and I know now that I must give myself into the service of it whatever it demands of me and wherever it leads. There will be years of waiting and wondering, but Palestine is not large and I shall need time to prepare and learn.

Hold me still in memory, my Tansar — this because one day, if the years be allowed us, I shall return to share with you what I shall be given. Now it is nameless, but one day I shall understand... Mark it well, my friend: some day, in the timeless plan of Ormuzd mediated through this one who is yet a child, our world of confusion will be translated into utter meaning.

If it be madness to give myself into such a loyalty and such a service, though as yet there is much to understand, then I am mad... Farewell...

Chapter 6

The Stable Boy

It seems strange that I should have been asked to write something of the Master's history. Surely, among all those who knew and loved him well, I am the least qualified to put down in effective words the mood and manner of his living.

And yet, this visitor among us, this Greek physician, has earnestly entreated me... You will deal kindly with my writing, remembering that it was late in life that I learned to write, and then only because the Master urged me to it.

Thus — my small contribution.

The story begins with my beginning — at Machaerus, the dustiest and most arid spot under heaven. By my time it had become what it is today: the most ungracious outpost in all the Roman empire. In case you are unfamiliar with my natal town, you should know that it lies in the lonely fastnesses of southern Perea some thirty leagues due east of the Dead Sea. A few of the Roman maps show it, I find, because of its supposed military importance as a garrison.

It was during an abortive insurrection in the early years of the Roman occupation of our town that my parents died at the hands of a drunken soldier. With no one to care, I became a boy of the streets, living by my wits. This proved to be a difficult existence: after the insurrection, the Roman government garrisoned Machaerus with men who were particularly brutal and sadistic. I've suspected since that our town became a penal colony of sorts for the military.

By the age of twelve I had myself become the hardest and most ruthless youngster on the streets. Having no reason to stay longer in Machaerus and several threatening reasons to leave, I departed late one hot morning with a passing camel train bound for the Passover market days in Jerusalem; the foreman needed an extra hand on the ropes.

It was to be a year, however, before I saw Jerusalem, and that in the company of a kindly Bethlehemite who had became my second father.

The camel train reached Bethlehem in late afternoon several days after our departure from Machaerus, and the foreman decided to stay the night. The innkeeper in the only hostelry the little town boasts was all bustle and confusion when our sizeable company descended on him without warning. It seemed that his stable boy had run off to the north the day before. The camels could forage in the grazing fields on the edge of town, but the horses should be watered and at least superficially curried; if we would be patient, he said, he would take care of our animals as quickly as he could.

Inwardly chafing at the delay of a night's stopover but having nothing better to do, and not choosing to traverse the remaining two leagues alone and in the night, I started to unpack the animals and stable the horses. I had become expert at this, thanks to the brutal demands of the jeering soldiers of Machaerus.

It was late before I had finished the task, but the underlying excitement of the trip had kept sleep away during much of our time on the dusty trade paths. As I knelt in my deep weariness to make a place in the hay to lie down, a voice close at hand said, "I can give you work if you'll stay."

I turned to see the innkeeper; he had been leaning against the stable gate watching me. His voice had kindness in it — the first personal kindness I could recall since the death of my parents.

"Don't lie there," he went on. "I'll fix a pallet in a corner of the common room for you. And — there's supper if you're hungry."

If I was hungry!... I couldn't remember not being hungry. I followed him to a table in the warm kitchen. While I consumed ladle after ladle of his hot stew, the innkeeper talked quietly to me; as are most men of his calling, he was expert at uncovering the past lives of his guests. My quick distrust of anyone I met began to dull and fade away under the influence of his quiet concern. Instinctively I liked him, and when he asked me to stay awhile and act as his stable boy until he could find a permanent replacement, I agreed.

He never did find a replacement, not for all the rest of his remaining years. Starved as my small body had been, it was my soul, my inner person, that was the more starved — for love and for someone to love. He too was lonely, and thus it was that we became as father and son.

My foster-father never wanted to turn any weary traveller away; I've seen him on many occasions give up his own room and sleep on the common room floor, so that a tired cameleer could rest comfortably. Failing this, I've seen him direct travellers to the innermost of our stables, cut deeply into the little hill that rises behind the inn. We rarely had use for it, and he had me keep clean straw there in case it was needed. He never accepted money for this. It occurred to me in later years that this was his way of observing the ancient law of the land of our people — the ungleaned portion of the farmer's crop to be left for the use of the passing stranger. This small stable was his ungleaned portion — for the welfare of the passing stranger.

The time passed with genuine happiness for me; I knew more contentment than in any other days I could remember. I scarcely noticed how they became weeks and then months.

Early in our relationship, my foster-father encouraged me to attend the synagogue school held by our village priest. At first I refused. I had no interest in the scrolls of our Scriptures; they were for boys who could afford to have dreams about the future. I had none; the cynicism early planted in me died away only slowly. One lived for the present day — nothing more; success meant that one went to bed without being hungry.

This nonsense about a God who cared... No such God would have allowed my father and mother to be killed at the hands of a Roman sergeant with a broad-sword in his hand.

Eventually I consented to go to the school, but it was at considerable personal sacrifice. For many months I disliked every moment of it.

It must have been two years and more that went by in this fashion. Then, quite suddenly, there was excitement in the air. It seemed that the Caesar — you will recall that Augustus was on the throne in those years — Augustus had decreed that all subject peoples in the eastern Roman colonies should be numbered and taxed. Further, in keeping with our ancient Palestinian taking of census according to tribe, family and house, people to be thus registered were to go to the central city of the tribe from which they were descended. This meant difficult demands of travel for many who could ill afford it, but it was the policy of Rome to make use of local custom wherever such custom did not work in opposition to the Empire. Rome always tried to appear the benevolent conqueror — whether this really meant trial and hardship for its colonies or not...

The census was to be completed within a set five-day period. As the ancestral center of the Davidic family — it has long been known as the "City of David" — our Bethlehem bustlingly prepared for the influx of people that we knew would be coming.

Traders from near and far set themselves to take advantage of the movement of population; caravan trains from the south and southeast bound for Jerusalem plodded past our inn door for weeks beforehand. Extra contingents of soldiers were transferred from Syria in the north to be on hand to prevent outbreaks or demonstrations. Altogether, what with long and slow-moving caravans, weary travellers coming to be enrolled, and the added soldiers everywhere, our dusty main street took on the look of a miniature metropolis.

Finally the appointed days were at hand. There was little rest or sleep for any of us at the inn. All day long and through much of the night, people were pounding on the inn door asking for lodging. Before mid-day, every day, all rooms were taken and I was worn to the bone with the need to care for and properly stable our guest's animals.

Most of the travellers who came to our door were well-dressed; my master felt it unfitting to mention the inner stable to many of them. The few to whom he did offer it rather stiffly refused.

On the fourth night of this bedlam, the train of events was initiated which was to change my life completely. It may seem strange that at the tender age of fourteen I would be set upon a totally new track. Here started the sequence of events which laid to rest the still cynical persona which had inwardly controlled me up to this critical point; it would begin in an inner stable of the Bethlehem inn, be nurtured in a small, dusty room of that inn, and finally be brought to full fruition by the most important human relationship of my life. The innkeeper who had become my foster-father said long afterward, as we talked it over and over again through the small hours of many a night, that it all happened because I had had a great need, and a Power far beyond the things of earth that had been my life up to that point — this Power had spoken to my need.

However you who read these words may choose to analyze the cause, the result was that I became hungry — hungry for many things that before I had only disdained...

To those of you who knew the man Jesus as Master or simply as "the Nazarene" in later life, this may not sound strange; such was always the way he affected men and women. He made them hungry for things of which they hadn't before felt any need. But that it should have happened to me, as a careless and hardened lad in dusty little Bethlehem — this is the most profound miracle I have ever witnessed. Nothing the Master did in after years seemed strange to me — in comparison with this.

Let me take you back to my story... This fourth night of the census began as usual. Hordes of people were walking the streets, soldiers were on patrol moving always in pairs, peddlers were hawking their wares. I had been forced to house several burros even in the innermost stable, the first time I had made use of it. I had completed the last feeding and watering and I had just stepped out the courtyard gate to stumble wearily to bed, when I saw them.

They were standing outside the main door talking to the innkeeper. I was surprised that he wasted time with them; we had literally *no* place for them — hadn't had since noon. A couple they were, young. The woman, seated on a small, tired burro, looked more weary than the animal. The young husband was telling the innkeeper something, standing close to him, and then I saw that kind man look at the woman with real concern in his eyes.

It was his responsibility, however, not mine. I started to brush past on my way to bed.

Taking my arm as I passed, the keeper stepped inside with me.

"Jonathan," he said, "make the inner stable ready for them."

"The inner — I can't," I said. "I was forced to put several burros in there."

"Surely there's some room."

"Yes," I said. "I didn't use all the stalls. But —"

"Do the best you can to find a clean stall, away from the animals. I've got to get some help. I'll bring these people back there myself shortly."

Then he was gone toward the common room, now crowded to capacity with travellers. It was the only time I ever remember his being peremptory with me.

Weary as I really was, I started to follow him in anger, thought better of it, turned back to the waiting couple. They were peasants; I guessed they were from the north country.

"Wait here," I said impatiently. "He'll be back. I've got to go and prepare some space in —" I looked at them — "in a stable." I waited for a reaction; there was none. I've often thought since with real humiliation of my condescending tone as I dismissed them and turned away.

The young man spoke, quite as though I were a grown-up.

"It's very good of you to trouble yourself on our account. You see — my wife is about to have a child."

A *child*. I looked at him with the sudden panic of the fourteen-year-old faced with something new and frightening. A baby... All of my hard boyhood years had never prepared me for this.

"Oh," I said. "Oh... Is she all right?"

He smiled then. "Yes, she's all right. Only — I think we'd best hurry."

I turned and ran toward the stables, I who a few moments before had felt I would never run again. I shooed cattle and burros and horses out of the way until, finally inside the far inner stable, I found a stall built against the back wall that was away from the animals.

In feverish haste I piled several armsful of fresh hay in one corner and threw a horse-blanket over the mound. I returned to the courtyard to find that the young man had tethered the burro meanwhile, and together we helped the woman out of the saddle. She smiled at me once, white-faced, and looking a little afraid.

Suddenly the courtyard seemed full of people. The innkeeper had bustled back followed by his wife and several others, including two women among his guests who had some experience in such things. I ran ahead, clearing the way among the animals, until we arrived at the far inner stable. We crowded into the stall I had prepared.

As quickly as he had appeared, my foster-father disappeared again. Without ceremony, I was pushed out into the next stable-section and a moment later the young father came after me. I wasn't sure whether I should go away and leave him alone... As I hesitated, my curiosity, the natural endowment of the young, swayed the balance; I stayed, throwing myself prone onto a mound of straw sloped against a manger. I was wide awake now.

The young man seemed disinclined to talk. First he paced back and forth, more nervous than he had allowed himself to appear before his wife. Then he stepped from the stable and disappeared into the night.

The moments dragged slowly by until an hour had passed and the young man had strolled back into the stable, looking less tense now.

Then it was that several things happened at once. The improvised curtain hanging before the inner stable was brushed aside and one of the women beckoned to the young man. He entered quickly. Uncertainly, I had risen to my feet; I was about to go in too, uninvited, when three cloaked figures appeared out of the gloom from the direction of the courtyard. They were simply-dressed men of the countryside, and then I saw by the staffs they carried that they were shepherds. I recognized one of them: they were from our local fields.

The men glanced about with indecision and then one of them saw me. He said, "We're looking for a baby..." His voice trailed off in uncertainty. Another one, older, advanced toward me, smiling quietly in recognition. We had chatted occasionally on the town square.

"We're looking for an infant king, and — we thought we might find him here." His voice was controlled as he made his strange inquiry and absorbed my confused stare.

I found my voice then. "I've not heard news of any king — especially here in the stable. None of our guests have spoken —"

I was interrupted by the curtain to the inner stable being brushed aside momentarily by someone within; light from the two candles inside flashed forth, then vanished again. The three shepherds pushed through at once, without ceremony or invitation; taking my chances, I slipped inside too. I crouched behind a water-trough from which I could see without being seen.

It didn't look as though there were very much to see. The young woman was lying on the pallet of hay I'd made for her, covered now by a blanket, and she was looking with curiosity at the figures just inside the doorway; the three had paused in some embarrassment. The young husband was standing close beside her, unsmiling and half protective in the presence of the strangers. The women who had come to help an hour before were frankly frightened; it was obvious that they wanted to escape.

I didn't notice the manger that had been pulled away from the wall until the oldest of the visitors stepped slowly and hesitantly over to it. The others joined him and they stood looking down into it, and then they looked at each other. I could see the face of one of them; he wore a queer expression, compounded of incredulity and a strange sort of certainty, as though he'd just made an important discovery.

It was then that without a word the leader knelt there in the dust beside the manger, and after a moment the others did, too. The older man's head was bowed frequently in prayer during what seemed to me, crouched behind the trough, to be a very long time.

No one said anything; I could hear one of the burros nearby loudly munching hay, and I had an odd impulse to go and hold its mouth still.

I was still contemplating this when I noticed that the three visitors had risen to their feet and were moving over to the pallet where the young mother lay. The older man took her hand and looked into her eyes; she smiled gently up at him.

"You are...blessed..." he said, and then the three of them turned and were gone.

The stable was quiet for a few moments, during which the young father came over to the water trough with a cup in his hand. I was trapped, but I didn't mind. I had to see what charm that manger held, to move so deeply such simple men as our local shepherds. Without thinking about it, I left my hiding place and strode softly forward.

The woman spoke to me then. "I've been wondering when you were going to come out from behind that trough and speak to us."

I felt color rising in my face. She wasn't laughing at me, though. Her smile came then, gentle and warm. For just a moment, a long-forgotten memory held me: I felt what boys feel who have a mother.

"May I — may I look?" I asked.

"Of course..."

I walked over to the manger. It held a sleeping baby, very pink and white, wrapped in a thick saddle-cloth. Nothing more...

I looked at the child in silence. There was no jewelry or finery to be seen; certainly there was no crown. I think I'd been expecting to see some sort of crown, since the shepherds had spoken of a young king.

Like most fourteen-year-olds, I didn't have much use for babies. That's all there was here — just a baby. Vaguely disappointed, I started to turn away.

Then, as though impelled by something outside of myself, I turned back and looked again. Nothing had changed — or had it? What was it? I felt suddenly frightened, and then calmed, and then — then it was as though an emptiness within me, a great void, had suddenly been filled. I can't describe it any other way.

The baby lay just as he had been, still asleep. But now I was gazing at him through tears — big fourteen-year-old tears — and I hadn't allowed myself to cry since I could remember. Crying was for boys who had someone to care about the crying.

I turned away and looked over at the woman then; her face was very serious and very concerned, and I knew that the concern was for me. Without thinking about it I ran over and threw myself down on the hay near her, and she put her hand in my hair and stroked it while I sobbed as though my heart would break.

Well... The young couple stayed with us for several weeks while the mother grew strong again. With the census now concluded and the crowds dispersed homeward again, within two days we moved them into a room in the inn where they could wait out their time in comfort. This was only "humane," as my foster-father put it.

It was only several days, however, after the child's birth that the little family again had visitors. I was sweeping the forecourt of the inn, my head down, when I almost swept the pointed boots of a tall figure that seemed to have appeared out of nowhere. He was dressed as I'd never seen anyone dressed, richly and colorfully, and he spoke to me from his considerable height in strongly accented speech.

"Where is he? Where is the infant king?" Here was that word again — king! The tall figure was joined immediately by two others dressed as colorfully as he, one swarthy and young, the other white with age.

"Well, speak up," said the tall stranger who had addressed me first. "Where is he? None of you townspeople seem to have tongues..."

My mind was working now, and I knew who — or rather what — these men were. I had heard them described on one or two occasions by travelling cameleers staying the night at our inn. They were from Babylonia, far to the east across a great desert, and they were wealthy. They spent their energies and lives in searching the sky for signs, watching the movement of the stars. They were called "Magi," which in our language simply means "Men of wisdom — wise men..."

I came to my senses to realize that they were looking around impatiently for someone else to direct them... The strange conduct of the shepherds four nights before flashed into my mind. They had knelt at the manger where the child of the peasant Nazarene couple had lain.

Could it be? A...king? I felt a chill run up my back.

I found my voice at last. "Sirs," I said, "I — I... come with me."

I led them into the inn and to the room where the young family was now housed in comfort. The tall visitor brushed aside the door-curtain without a word and disappeared inside, the other two following.

I heard later from the young mother what had happened. Apparently the three Magi came into the room and without a glance at the young couple, strode to the small cradle we had improvised in one corner of the room; they stood looking into it for some time and talking in low tones in their strange tongue. One of them suddenly called out what must have been an order to servants in the hall, who returned in a few minutes with three small chests. Then, amazingly, these men of wealth and learning knelt on the dirt floor of the silent room — knelt before the cradle, mind you — and each placed his box in the manner of an offering of fealty to a king, on the floor beside the sleeping child.

They remained on their knees for several minutes. It was not as though they were in prayer, the young mother told me later. Their attention was focussed upon the sleeping child, utterly and to the exclusion of all else.

At length, one after another, they rose to their feet. The first to move came to the pallet on which the young woman lay; standing quietly beside her, he bowed his head. Then, straightening to his full height and looking down at her, he said in heavily accented speech, "Favored are you among women. You are surely the mother of a king."

Without another word, their robes rustling, the three men strode from the room and from the inn. They remained only a day or two in their rich encampment on the edge of the town and then they were gone.

In the days that followed I continued to grow closer in affection to the young couple and their child. The young mother never spoke further of the Magi, nor did I. Just once, on the morning following, she had told me what occurred during the visit of the strange men to her room; I marvelled at her words then, and I've not ceased to marvel since.

I was with the young couple as constantly as my duties would permit; several times I sat by the child, alone with him while he sunned in the late mornings.

The young family left us quite suddenly one afternoon, travelling hurriedly to the southward. This worried me until, some months later, we received a brief note from the young husband. They had travelled all the way to Egypt, had dwelt there for awhile, and then had travelled back again and on north to their home in Nazareth in the hills west of the Sea of Galilee. The note ended with more than an invitation; it was a request to visit them.

We did visit them, though it was a five days' journey. More, we visited them twice each year thereafter as long as my adopted father lived.

This is not the place to record the long history of my friendship with him who became my Master and my Lord, who these twenty years past gave himself for me as he has for all people who learn to love him and to need him.

To need him... This is what it was on that night of the census so long ago now. I had a great need; always I had felt it. I had also a deep sense of loyalty, of fealty, a thirsting to serve, a longing to throw myself into the service of something or someone — someone who would understand me and take me for what I was, and need me, and love me even as I poured out my love in return. All of this was in me, a part of me, but my years as a brutalized child had buffeted it and bruised it and almost killed it within me. God had seemed far away, an empty dream, and the world a hard and cold place.

Then, without preamble, stumbling into one event after another in those fateful days of the great census, I had found the answer to all my need. Without the experience to analyze the matter, I yet sensed what I had discovered, knew its value. This is why there at the manger it was as though a void within me had suddenly been filled.

Surely it wasn't anything the child lying there asleep had done to me. It was simply what God did through the child...

Those of you who were close to the Master during his years among us will understand my experience. All of us who were in spiritual need, and who felt that need, could be filled with the wonder and certainty of God which worked through the Master — whether he himself as the medium, or the channel, or the revelation, was standing talking to us on the slope of a Galilean hillside or was lying, a tiny child, in a manger.

It didn't matter. It didn't matter because God was in Christ, working through him uniquely. God was always in Christ working through him. The power of God is not limited, held in, by the age or condition of its channel if God chooses to speak and act.

God was in Christ always — in the baby Jesus just as he was in the man. I know. I know because he found me and filled me as I stood in a Bethlehem stable by a manger that was also a cradle.

BOOK TWO

The Witnesses at Calvary

Chapter 1

Once I Was Blind

His name was Judas. He was one of the twelve disciples of our Master, up almost to the end. Then, just before the end, he stumbled and Christian history since has disdained his memory.

But — one wonders about Judas...

There is a persistent tradition that Judas was an educated man. We are told that when it was all over, he went out and hung himself. Before doing so, though, like other literate and passionate people, Judas would have left some word, perhaps a letter to those who had been his companions...

Peter, I am writing this to you. You will find me in the morning, and it will be soon enough. Even though you spurn my name and call me the betrayer, you will come despite your new rejection of me. I will send a message to you and your curiosity will bring you here. Oh, I know you well, Peter...

It won't be a pleasant experience for you, and this I regret. Below my body, though, as it hangs from the gnarled old limb curving above my head even now, pointing a prophetic finger to the skies — you will find, on this grey rock upon which I've been sitting, the pages I have written during these long hours before dawn. You can't read, Peter, but you will recognize my handwriting, and you will hurry with the pages to Matthew — oh yes, Peter, how well I know you! — and you will listen avidly as Matthew reads them to you, and I hope to the others as well.

Recall that I was never really one of you, Peter. I tried so often to think and dream like a Galilean peasant — forgive me, Friend — but I couldn't ever quite accomplish it. You Northerners have a different accent to your speech and to your wit.

More than this, though, I had committed the sin of learning how to read and how to write. Most of you knew only how to fish, and so you turned from me, all of you.

I never told you much about myself, Peter. It is enough now to say that my family had been wealthy once; when I came along there was a little left, enough to send me up from our dusty Kerioth to the great city for higher training under the temple teachers.

I couldn't find myself even there. No calling which presented itself attracted me, and I took to long walks, sometimes tramping northward or eastward for two and three days at a time, hoping that in the exercise and the healthy fatigue, if not in something that I should come up against along the way, I would find myself and the direction of my life.

The discovery, when it came, was unexpected...

I had gone down to Jericho on this occasion, had crossed the Jordan just beyond, and had turned northward up the east bank to tramp the river road toward the Decapolis. It was noon of the third day that I came upon him, speaking to a group of people on a hill overlooking the Jordan Valley some distance south of Galilee.

I wasn't in the mood for a lecture but I was hungry, and I had been alone for two days. I threw myself onto the grass and unlaced my rucksack for a biscuit and some dried mutton that I carried. The road up the hill had been steep and the day was hot.

I tried to enjoy the view and not listen to him, but he was saying what for me then were the most astonishing and audacious things I had ever heard. Travelling preachers are plentiful enough, but it was obvious inside of three minutes that here was a refreshingly original thinker.

I moved closer. He sat on a large stone, comfortable, at ease; the phrase which accurately describes his manner sounds odd, but I can only say it: *he spoke with relaxed realism.* It was a manner which wove an aura of authority about whatever he said.

After the crowd had dispersed I went up to question him further on some of his points of philosophy. It was this "peace" business that particularly caught my attention — not that I believed it for a moment... Surely this fellow knew that as a nation it was necessary for us to win the right to peace — by throwing off the Roman yoke. I had thought this view was so common that no one ever questioned it.

Yet the longer I talked with him the more fascinated I became and the more lost in that amazing magnetism of his. I hardly noticed when he sat down on his rock again and I threw myself onto the grass at his side, and we talked and talked. He ignored the rest of you completely for over an hour, didn't he, Peter, while the sun waned to the westward and you stood first on one foot and then another.

The upshot, of course, was that he needed someone like me. He was building a school of disciples, he said, and someone was needed to watch over the practicalities — to arrange for food, for nights lodgings, to see that there was some sort of financial stability to the thing. Would I spend awhile with them? The others lacked the knowledge and experience, he said. I considered; no one in Jerusalem or elsewhere was waiting for me or needing me... and he fascinated me.

So it was that I accepted a place in his company — just for a few weeks, of course... A few weeks? No one could be a member of his band for a short while and then pull away, could they, Peter — not if he had chosen them to stay.

It was so wonderful, so idyllic at first. I knew that some of the rest of you were jealous of me because Jesus and I talked on a different plane from his conversations with you. First I was intrigued, then captivated — and finally I grew to love him as a man, a thinker, a leader quite as much as the rest of you.

It was a point of pride with me to take care of things. The wealthy circles in Jerusalem who make such a point of contributing funds to travelling preachers and their bands had to be approached with tact; more broadly, the ever larger crowds who came to hear the Master learned where I would be standing with my bag in my hand as they left for home.

Everything we did had its center in Jesus as a person — as, for me, the Messiah...

Yes, Peter — you began to feel it too. Long before he voiced his approval of you for putting it into words that day on the road to Caesarea, we all sensed the strange destiny that was before him. As you know only too well, it was so easy for us to forget his words about the peacemakers and the blessed meek...

Within a year, I was sure that he was preparing to proclaim himself publicly the Messiah. Educated as I was, and careful with the money, it was clear that my future was tied closely to his. He would need me more than any of the rest of you, I thought; his Chancellor — that is what I would be.

I have no shame in admitting here how my imagination ran on. The Master was so kingly, so unconsciously regal in bearing and personality. Oh, it was easy to dream.

I realized later that this is when the change began to come...

It was about the middle of our second year with him, I believe. One day I had been sitting on a rock away from the crowd while he spoke to it, I remember, and did some of those amazing things he could do with people's personal needs if they believed enough in him. I was dreaming — a bit selfishly, I'm afraid. I was looking off to the south toward where Jerusalem lay; I couldn't see the city but I knew about where it would be, sheltered in the hills there below the skyline... His Chancellor, yes; with him I would plan the accounts and budget for the whole nation, and they would all be waiting on me for advice and favors...

Oh, don't condemn me, Peter. You were all the same... What began to bother me, though, was that when I looked back over the dispersing crowd late in the day, there was the Master walking off with you and James and John — the "holy three" I began to call you in my own mind with gathering bitterness. Why should he choose you? He had me, and frankly, we had much more to talk about, Jesus and I, than he could find for discussion when he was with you.

This is the only starting-point upon which I can put my finger as I think back. The matter began to grow up in my mind and it further put me off, away from the rest of you. You had raised your wall against me long since, but now, in my growing jealousy, I raised my wall too.

I wasn't alone in my dreams of grandeur, Peter, as you well know. There was the day, for instance, when James and John, hiding behind the skirts of their mother, came to the Master and had her ask that when he announced himself and took control of the kingdom, her two sons could sit on either side of his throne — be his vice-rulers, nothing less!

Later, when I remonstrated with him about it in considerable heat, Jesus reacted in the exasperating way that was so habitual with him: he made me see the real reason for the anger I had felt, I and the rest of us, Peter. You felt it too... I saw the flush rising on your face as the mother was speaking to Jesus.

Inwardly, we were all grasping for the same prize. Each of us wanted to sit at the Master's side when he came to his throne... only I most of all, Peter, and I had just cause. I was educated, I was almost as young as the rest of you and as strong; further, I had abilities and training to bring to the Master's service — which is more than the rest of you had.

It becomes clear as I look back that my relationship with the Master deteriorated rather rapidly after that. I couldn't take him on the same simple and unquestioning terms as the rest of you: I simply couldn't. I knew too much — too much history, too much philosophy, too much of what it would take to overthrow Rome — and he wasn't getting at it. He was making no preparations. He wasn't busy with the influential friends who would help us when the time came.

You didn't care, because you didn't know the paths that had to be followed. I did, and I worried and fretted — though never aloud, to him, because he had forbade me ever to speak of such things in his presence... Thus it was that I bore it all in silence — and grew more and more morose, I suppose.

To add to it all, the Master kept choosing you and James and John for his confidences. The others were so lost in their rosy love for him that they didn't care — but I did. I was the one who had much in common with him. I was the one who knew what he ought to be doing, and he wouldn't listen. In time, he no longer confided in me as he did in you Holy Three.

As our third year with him wore on, he became increasingly prodigal with money. This drove me nearly wild, and as usual he had no ear for me when I remonstrated.

Then one day, the Master presented us each with a small portion of silver for ourselves. I have no idea where he had put hands on it, and just this one time he did it. It changed my perspective and pulled me up from my slough of despond: I felt that his hour was shortly to be at hand — the hour when he would publicly proclaim himself. I purchased this small field with my share; I'd need it for my palace when the great day came, and the tree on it is a magnificent thing.

The tree... I'm sitting in its shadow now, Peter, as the early morning sun rises higher. My tree it is, and soon it will take from me my life...

My hopes of grandeur, though, were short-lived. The Master kept asking for the bag and taking from it money that I had been hoarding for days; he would then give it to any dirty beggar that came to him in need. He worried sympathetically and openly about prostitutes that we would meet and lepers and other useless scum of the streets.

This was no way to come into power. What was the matter with him? His fame and popularity in these late days were clear for all to see. He had everything on his side: if he'd just raised a finger, a thousand men would have jumped to his banner and we would have been on our way.

But no...he wouldn't save the funds that found their way to us, popular now as he was; property meant nothing to him. He refused to meet the right people or talk with them; he had the most exasperating way of insulting most of the wealthy and influential Pharisees who might have helped us when the great day came.

Through all of this I became mare confused and puzzled by him, more hurt, more jealous of you Holy Three, and so more aloof. I was as unhappy as I'd ever been in my life — and all because I loved him so. Here was the kernel of my problem. I couldn't walk off and leave him and throw up the whole thing, because I loved him so.

Without warning, two things happened that completed my downfall. I was lifted to the heights with hope and then thrown down in utter despair.

We finally turned toward Jerusalem.

The others of you were worried about our going there, but I was sure I knew why he was doing it; on that day following the Sabbath, I was positive that I had guessed right. In complete joy, a joy rescued from a long despair, I sang and laughed and rejoiced with the others as we escorted the Master into the city riding that small white colt we'd borrowed for him. I could barely wait until we arrived at the temple steps.

This was it, after all of our struggle and doubting and waiting! He had come into the city as our prophets had *said* the Messiah would — riding a colt. We had no money and few friends, but evidently the Master knew what he was doing. He was going to proclaim himself at last... It would be impossible to describe to you my absolute, unbounded relief and joy.

Then we arrived...and dumfounded, I heard him tell the people to go away, that he wouldn't be their king. *He wouldn't be their king...*

I didn't know what to say or do, or to whom to turn. The next few days are a blur in my memory. I was so utterly undone that I was hardly conscious of people or activity around me. My memory of this period is simply a void.

My recollection returns with our dinner in the home of Simon the Leper there in Bethany, and after dinner came that simpering woman who poured a whole jar of the most expensive perfume she could find over his head — his *head*, mind you... There was I with our purse well-nigh flat against my thigh; that jar of perfume, if sold, might have been a fresh nest-egg for a new beginning. But no: she had to scent the hot room up like a queen's bower — pour a king's ransom on his head!

I began to expostulate, and he cut me off abruptly. It was the only time I ever recall his being publicly sharp with me. He actually praised her for what she had done...

Seething, I arose from the table and hurried out into the night. The air was cool, but I didn't feel the coolness. I was very close to hating him then, hating his whole confused, illogical conduct — none of which I could fathom.

I didn't hate him, though, Peter. I loved him and I wanted to help him see the way, and I couldn't: he wouldn't listen, wouldn't let me talk about it, wouldn't let me suggest what he might do. I paced furiously along the rutted street.

Then — as I walked, suddenly I saw it.

I saw what I could do. It would take nerve, a great deal of nerve, but I would never make him see and act without taking such a chance... I would force his hand. I would *make* him declare himself. I would put him into a position from which there could be no more of these sentimental retreats of his...

The rest of you would hate me temporarily, but I couldn't see that you liked me much as it was.

I knew exactly to whom to go; I knew them all, well. After all, I had been their student just a few years before. I hurried toward the temple, and the cool air broke through to me as my anger slowly subsided in a vast surge of hope.

Thus my story bends toward its end... You see why I did it, Peter. I didn't give a fig for their money; did you really think I would sell my Master and see him condemned for thirty paltry pieces of their temple silver?

I knew they would welcome me, though, which they did. Further, I knew they hated him and longed to trap him, which they did. They accepted my plan with enthusiasm.

That kissing part, Peter: I hated and shrank from it. It doesn't matter whether you believe this; I'll soon be beyond your power to hate or to love... But the kiss was necessary to make things look right. I had to overdo it, or they might have suspected.

After all, he was the Messiah. He was going to have to declare himself now, and he would probably put them all out of office and put us in their places, and I couldn't afford to let them catch even an inkling of what was to happen. When I kissed him, it would be with a strange inward mixture of anticipation and recoil.

Then the deed was done, there in the garden in the cool moonlight. They roughly took him prisoner — and I held my breath in enraptured anticipation, waiting for him with lordly gesture to throw off their hands and call fire down upon them from heaven for daring to touch the Messiah...

My feet turned suddenly icy cold in the wet grass; my heart almost ceased beating... He didn't do it. He didn't do anything. He simply let them take him away — a prisoner.

As one in a trance, I trudged back with the soldiers and temple underlings who had come out a dissolute mob to take him. First to the house of crafty old Annas we went; later, moving with the crowd, I realized we were clustering into the audience chamber of Caiaphus, the High Priest. I knew him well. He saw me in the crowd, looked quickly away and said nothing; with a shock I realized that even he despised me now as a betrayer, an informer.

Peter, I wonder if you can imagine the depth of my turmoil of soul... It had all been so sure, so foolproof; I couldn't see how it could fail — but it had. I knew it now, as surely as I knew I was standing there.

Out of my sense of tragic failure began to emerge a gripping, awful realization of what was happening. They were twisting everything the Master had said and done recently to make it all sound first like blasphemy and then like treason against Roman authority. Finally I heard them pronounce recommendation of death — death!... And I had thought he was the Messiah...

Even then I had a moment of wild hope. Surely he wouldn't allow himself to be murdered. You've seen him heal the sick, Peter, and even bring a man alive out of the tomb. If you had been inside that night with me, could you believe that he would allow plotters to take his life?

But no... For awhile, he wouldn't say anything. When he did speak, it was only to give them more grist for their mill.

My horror mounted...

Suddenly, it was as though something long taut within me broke. All of my defenses came crashing down, and in a flash of shocked understanding, I saw. My self-centered, merciful blindness was over. Suddenly I saw...

My selfish dreams, my terrible failure in seeking to plot my Master's future, my refusal to accept things on his terms and my fatal insistence on bending him to *my* terms — I saw it all, in brilliant clarity and with a numbing sense of loss.

Then, fast on the heels of this came a vision of the enormity of my betrayal of him. He couldn't save himself; he couldn't — and still be true to himself.

I knew him, had known him well enough to see all of this... Of course! How could I have been so selfishly blind, so disastrously obdurate? I — *I had given him up to death...*

You will never know, any of you, the awful hell which suddenly engulfed me.

Then, as I stood in the crowd almost in shock, the most shattering thing of all happened... As you well know, Peter, the Master often knows what we are thinking before we speak, not through any sorcery but simply because he is more conscious of the need of others, particularly those close to him, than he is of his own need.

I thought of all of this later. It has been a long night here in my little piece of earth, my field...

As I've said, I suddenly saw in a flash the whole terrible sequence — my own mistake, his absolute justification, and my infamy. It was as though I had cried out in my anguish, although I hadn't uttered a sound. But it was enough...

I was looking at him, and without preamble he turned a third of the way around, so still had he been standing while the close-packed mob howled around him — he turned and his eyes sought me out. This I shall never make you believe, but it no longer matters: he looked me in the eyes across the heads of the crowd, precisely as he had done so long before on a sunny afternoon near the Jordan when I had first seen him. There was warmth there, and understanding, and tenderness and acceptance of me. He accepted me again — he accepted *me.*

It only lasted a moment before someone jerked him roughly around, but it was enough. I felt suddenly sick, pushed my way panic-stricken through the crowd to a side-entrance, and hurried out into the cobbled alley. I was utterly alone, untouchable. I had no one...no one.

No one? Strangest fact: there is one who will not join the chorus of rejection, and only one: the man I have betrayed.

I know that he must die, although I don't know how or when; since leaving him there in the mob, I've been here alone. But such goodness as his the world cannot abide...

Peter, my night of suffering is past. In a single cluster of hours I have grown through the years I shall never see...this, because I know now what he meant when he said that we must accept his kingdom as a little child. I used to shake my head at that, determined not to understand... Truly, once I was blind.

What is important to Jesus is not justification, but transfiguration: not honor and position and security in this world, not fame and fortune, not that we should become kings — but sons, fit to be the sons of the kind of God he kept telling us about...when we would listen, and stop dreaming our dreams of conquest.

He has known all along, Peter, that he is going to die, and soon: he is aware that people will not face for long the silently accusing finger of his complete righteousness.

But you see, the Master has never allowed the specter of death to move him far from his chosen track. In the place to which he is going, he said once, are many houses. He used the word with love: he meant it to sound warm and companionate, like a home — like the home I've not known since boyhood years.

I will now, though, Peter. I am going home — because when he looked at me last night across the heads of the gathered mob, he was taking me again, accepting me. He was promising me that I, too, will meet him there, that there will be a place for me — for me, his betrayer.

Oh, how I have come to see reality and truth this night. Once I was blind, but now I see...

Peter, if Jesus, our Master, is what and whom I believe him to be, I have committed a deed which future centuries will neither forget nor condone. But — even this is not too much for the love of a fatherly God, a God whose son, whose mediating voice upon earth, Jesus claims to be.

Peter, if me — if he accepts *me*, then surely all people...

My time has come. Those children up there on the road are enjoying the flowers — my flowers. I must get the youngsters away, though; right now I have use for my field, my tree. I'll give the children these last coins and send them into the city to find you, Peter.

These coins... Strange... I was given them two days ago by a first sergeant out of Pilate's guard. He had seen my tree, and he paid these pence for two of its heavier limbs. He remarked that there is a hurried need for a third cross. In addition to two thieves sentenced to death a month ago and to be crucified today, the governor has decreed yet a third crucifixion. It is to be a robber named — Barabbas, I believe he said.

Chapter 2

Letters From Simon

Personal correspondence... From the historian's standpoint, it can be fascinating and revealing...

In a North African dig near Alexandria some years ago, an ancient, well-crafted box of a size to fit onto a table or desk and carefully wrapped in what seems originally to have been camel's skin, was uncovered. Lying amidst a closely-packed cache of other personal articles, it had been providentially spared from much of the action of the elements. Among other surprising details of the small find was the fact that it contained a series of letters written, amazingly, in Aramaic — a first-century hybrid text usually associated with the eastern shore of the Mediterranean rather than North Africa. Scholarly opinions vary somewhat as to certain details, but some broad facts are revealed in the letters which are generally undisputed.

The writer made a voyage to Jerusalem from what today we call Libya about 2,000 years ago. Making the difficult trip in order to be on hand for the celebration of one of the great days in the Jewish calendar, the Feast of the Passover, he broke into the Christian Gospel writings by a strange occurrence which he would gladly have avoided. A comment he makes at one point in his letters indicates that, like many Africans, he was dark of skin; he was apparently a man of some means, and it seems clear that he was a devout man, a Jew deeply and sincerely. His two sons Rufus and Alexander are mentioned in the gospels, evidence that they must later have became part of the early Christian community.

The name he gives is simply Simon, and he was a resident of Cyrene, near the coast. The letters were written to his wife, whom apparently he loved deeply; they were sent to her during the first days of his visit in the Jewish capital. The present translation is considered accurate; it is recent and purposely colloquial.

The earliest letter in the group was dictated to a local scribe — hence the use of Judean Aramaic — on the afternoon of the fifth day of the week, just a day before that annual occasion on which Jews gather for the evening Passover feast about the Paschal Lamb.

* * *

My Miriam,

It was pleasant to arrive at the country estate of my old friend Eleazar after the confining trip. God granted us fine weather for the voyage and I found the captain stimulating company. The winds were provident most of the way, and except for two days of calm not far off the Judean coast, all went well.

Joppa is a fascinating seaport. Seamen are everywhere about the streets, and it was only with difficulty that I was able to obtain a mount and a pack-animal for the journey to Jerusalem.

On my arrival at Eleazar's country home just an hour's easy walk from one of the main gates of the city, I found myself guest in a supremely pleasant abode. Eleazar's love of life's good comforts and bodily ease would allow him to live no other way.

This morning I took early leave of my host and tramped alone through the hills toward the Damascus Gate in the North Wall. Rounding a bend in the road, suddenly I saw the city there before me, shining in all the glory of the early morning sun. A little valley lay between my road, along the upper edge of a garden they call Gethsemane, and the city wall beyond; the towers and domes of the metropolis were exposed clearly and distinctly.

I stood there for many minutes, drinking in the beauty and splendor of the view. I have never seen Rome upon its seven hills, but I am sure it could not be as commanding a sight.

At length I resumed my journey, and in a few minutes I found myself within the city. People are everywhere, selling or buying, seeing the sights, visiting the famous places and the numerous shrines of our faith. It is all very colorful and fascinating and noisy. Tell my sons that one of these years, when they are old enough to withstand the rigors of travel, we shall come up to the Holy City together. Tell Rufus that I saw a huge, milk-white horse today; a shaggy-bearded trader from far across the Jordan was riding him cockily, like a rooster.

My love to you.

Simon

* * *

My Miriam,

Scarcely am I in a condition to think clearly. Surely I cannot explain coherently what happened to me this morning... It is now an hour past noon, and I have hurried to dispatch this word to you. Never have I been so confused and so angry.

Yet usual words fall short and lax. What I feel is something both less and more than mere anger...

I left Eleazar's house again early this morning; yesterday I had only begun to see all the things that this most amazing of cities contains, and I had much to do. I had almost reached the Damascus Gate again when I saw that the road was blocked. It must have been shortly after eight o'clock; people entering the city had met a large crowd moving outward and temporarily the gate was clogged.

As we stood waiting, it became evident that the people coming out were not merely strangers searching out famous and holy places. A crowd — almost a mob — of local folk surrounded a squad of Roman soldiers with some prisoners in hand. There was nothing to do but wait until they had passed by.

I must say, Miriam, that I was entirely incurious. All I wished was to get through the gate and into the city. Though I pitied the prisoners when I saw that they were dragging each one a cross — you know what this means under current Roman law — still, the condemned no doubt deserved what they were about to receive. I thought so then and I think so now — at least...well, let me tell you what happened.

I was standing waiting for the procession to go by; there were three prisoners, each surrounded by four soldiers. Two of the prisoners had passed where I was standing; the crowd was pressed close about, and though we were outside the gate the street was not wide.

The third prisoner was clearly more weary than the others. He was moving slowly and he couldn't have gone much farther anyway...

Why he had to choose to fall to the ground right in front of me I'll never know, but that's just what he did — fainted dead away and crumpled face forward into the dust of the street.

The crowd murmured sympathetically and the officer in charge tried to rouse him by shaking his shoulder. When there was no response, the officer — a very young centurion he was — looked about him with a rather baffled air. Some of the rougher men present grinned; I suppose it was an embarrassing predicament for an inexperienced Roman officer.

Obviously, he was looking for someone else to drag the cross. He didn't dare ask any of the local Jews present; they had cleansed themselves for the feast and they would have caused him no end of trouble with his superiors. I, too, had cleansed myself; I felt reasonably safe.

Miriam, what words can describe the feeling that came over me when the centurion stepped up and put a hand on my shoulder. He spoke quietly, but with authority.

"You!" he commanded. "Carry the cross for him." The crowd melted away from around us as I started to protest.

"I am a Jew..."

I suppose it was the darkness of my skin, Miriam, that marked me an outsider. At any rate, the centurion's hand went to his dagger scabbard and I saw that protest would be futile and could be dangerous.

Anger welled up in me, black and unreasoning, and hatred — hatred of this weakling of a prisoner who couldn't take his just deserts like a man. I stepped forward, dressed as I was — I knew no one in the crowd to whom I could hand my good tunic — and kneeling in the dirt I picked up the cross. They had only bound the two beams together — they planned to nail them later — but the burden was difficult to manage.

I didn't even look at the criminal there on his face; some in the crowd were snickering at my discomfiture... Miriam, if I live forever I shall never again know such stinging rage. I discovered later that there had been tears in my eyes — tears of humiliation and anger.

As I moved off with the cross, the prisoner, conscious again, was lifted onto his feet. I walked a few steps and then stopped to wait for the soldiers. The crowd had fallen suddenly silent; I looked back.

The prisoner, supported by one of the soldiers, was speaking to a little group of women. It didn't make sense...

In less than a minute the squad came on toward me and I moved ahead. The two prisoners in front of us had disappeared around a curve but groups of curious people lined the roadside as far as I could see. The pace quickened a little and I realized that the condemned man was walking by himself now, just a step or two behind me.

I suppose we had been on the way for five minutes or so when he spoke to me.

"I'm sorry," he said. "I know this is putting you to embarrassment and trouble."

I was about to tell him to hold his tongue, thought better of it, said nothing. We moved slowly on. Finally we paused at the foot of a beetle-browed hill up which a side road wound steeply; we had just turned onto it.

This time the man touched me on the shoulder.

"Thank you," he said. "I think I can manage it now."

I put down the cross and began to straighten my tunic. Without much curiosity, I looked at him.

Miriam, it sounds less than sane, but since that moment I haven't been able to think clearly about this whole experience. It has had a queer unearthliness about it, and yet not in any unpleasant or superstitious way... Perhaps I can describe it better a bit later; as you can see, I am confused...

I saw for the first time why he had fainted. They had been pretty rough with him. He had been whipped with lead-weighted thongs and he'd lost a lot of blood. For some reason his forehead was matted with freshly-clotted scratches and cuts. He looked completely exhausted — been up all night, I guessed.

But — it was his eyes that did it. I know this sounds incredible, Miriam, but when he looked at me *I felt as if he owned me*. I can't express it any other way. There was kindness there, and a deep understanding of what I was going through... Imagine! He was facing *death*, but he was feeling compassion for my embarrassment.

There was more. Although he wasn't smiling, there was an impression of warmth showing through, almost of camaraderie... But Miriam, how was I to deal with it — the strange feeling that this man owned me, this criminal about to be executed?

As I said earlier, his eyes did it. I picked up the cross again.

"I'll carry it up the hill for you," I said, trying to sound unconcerned; my voice quivered in mid-sentence. "Anyway," I said, "you look tired."

At that, he actually smiled. “Thank you,” he said. “You’re very kind.”

In that moment, Miriam, I said the strangest thing I have ever said in my life. I don’t know why I said it. That odd feeling that this man owned me came rolling over me again.

“No, I’m not being kind,” I said. “I *want* to carry it for you.”

We went on up the hill. The prisoner walked beside me in silence. At the top, the unpleasant business of execution was already in progress on the other two of the condemned; I will spare you, my dear, any word of the horror I beheld...

As we arrived they were raising the first cross. I laid down my burden and turned. The man was looking at me. Again, that odd feeling of being owned came over me, and there was no opposing feeling of resentment; I can only say that it all seemed strangely right — and genuine.

He put out his hand. I thought he was going to touch me, but after a moment he dropped his hand to his side. Again he smiled, and once more that odd feeling came over me of warmth, of comradeship.

Then he said quietly, “God has blessed you for this.”

Miriam, note the words: not “May God bless you” — not even “God will bless you.” It was simply a plain statement: “God has blessed you for this.”

I looked at him, looked into his eyes, and suddenly, to cap all the strange things that had happened, I felt choked and knew that I was about to break into weeping... I, Miriam, who consider myself a hard man — I was about to weep... I wheeled around, broke through the surrounding lines of people, and began to run back along the hill road, down and down.

You will find it hard to believe, Miriam, but I was sobbing before I had freed myself of the crowd, weeping without control all the way down that wild, running descent — and all of it over a man whom I had never seen before that very hour.

At the bottom of the hill there stood a single burly figure; he waved for me to stop, and when I made as if to rush by him he put out a muscular arm and pulled me off my feet. He turned about to look at me, still holding me in that vice-like grip.

“Speak!” he said. “Is he on the cross?”

"They're doing it now," I said, and tried to pull free. His grip tightened.

"You're weeping," he said. "Why?"

Then he let me go and answered his own question.

"Ah, I know... This morning I wept too. Now I can't; I'm beyond it... He once called me 'Petras,' his rock. This morning I became mere Simon again."

"Simon?" I said. "That's my name, too."

He didn't seem to hear me. Turning on his heel he spoke over his shoulder. "Come to the house of Helena if you'd like, later." Then he was gone, up the hill road.

I turned toward the city. I had to gain control of myself. The road was almost empty as I strode toward the great gate. I entered, and I have been walking ever since about the city, aimlessly. It is now well after the noon hour.

Miriam, I can explain this only very poorly now. Perhaps tomorrow I shall be able to do better. The city has been busy with its Passover ceremonials and I hear no reference at all to what occurred this morning on the hill beyond the wall. Most people know or care nothing about it apparently.

I am confused and distraught. The man was a common criminal; that should be an end to it. But Miriam — it isn't...

All of this, I know, must sound to you as though I've gone suddenly out of my mind. Certainly I am in deep confusion. I must dispatch this immediately.

Simon.

* * *

My Miriam,

It is the Sabbath. At the temple today the press of the crowd was unbearable. The liturgy meant nothing to me. I have been all day as one in a trance.

My scribe knows of a Helena who lives near a market square off the street called Straight. Perhaps this is the one mentioned by the burly Simon who took me in arm yesterday at the foot of the hill.

I seem to have lost touch with my essential self. Nothing clarifies. I have had no sleep this past night: am I really out of my mind? At times I am sure of it.

Who was the criminal whose cross I carried? Who was he? No one seems to know or particularly to care. My turmoil I can share with none here; Eleazar would simply laugh and offer to refill my wine cup.

Yet it is not really curiosity which so confounds me. I care little as to who the man was. But — what has he done to me? What is his spell? God help me!

Simon.

* * *

My Miriam,

It is the first day of the week. I have found the beginning of an answer to the maddening turmoil by which I've been gripped — but it's an answer so strange that I scarcely dare tell you of it.

First I must explain that early in this afternoon I went to the house of Helena near the Straight Street. Simon came to the door — the same Simon it was who so roughly stopped me on the hill road. There was no light of recognition in his eye at first, and then suddenly he remembered.

"You!" he said, and I think he smiled. He took my arm, pulled me into the house, closed the door with one large foot and propelled me into the central chamber. Some of the people within were speaking tensely and excitedly to others, and two or three were sitting motionless on their benches. But Miriam — never have I seen such gladness on human faces as was written upon these.

Simon led me to one who was introduced as Helena, our hostess. She looked at me, and her eyes widened as she spoke.

"You are the one who carried his cross!"

The events of the past days had been almost too much for me. My face must suddenly have drained its color. Seeing my need of air, Simon took me with him to the upper roof-platform of the house and I have been there with him to this evening hour.

Miriam, there is no way by which I can prepare you for what Simon has said to me, or Peter, as those of this household call him — has said to me and has well-nigh made me believe. I can merely tell you: Peter's claim and his deathless conviction is that this man who was crucified was none other than the Messiah who, as he says it, came to seek and to save to a life everlasting those who call upon his name.

There it is. I've told you. Would that you could have been at my side during these afternoon hours on the house-top.

The things that this crucified prisoner did and said, as Peter repeated them to me, have spoken both to my mind and my heart with the ring of truth. I am forced to choose between two irreducible facts: either the man whose cross I carried was an insane genius, or he was indeed somehow the person of a loving God in human flesh...

Miriam, believe in me until I see you again. I know you will find it difficult, but believe in me — for I must tell you of Peter's further claim: this man, whose name was Jesus from the upcountry hamlet of Nazareth and who was crucified on the hill and buried two days ago — *this man has disappeared from the tomb in which he was laid*, despite the seal of the Emperor on the rolling-stone and a guard of Roman soldiers on watch just outside... Word came this morning and Peter himself went to investigate.

There is that in me which cries against all these claims; there is much here which goes against the logic of things known and trusted.

There is that in me also which reminds me of a level of being which embraces yet exceeds logic: the level of the spirit. This man Jesus apparently spoke constantly of such a reality.

Miriam, believe in me. I am fighting for my sanity. Tomorrow Peter promises to take me to see the tomb. Believe in me.

Simon

* * *

My Miriam,

The battle is over. The conflict has ceased.

This morning I went with Peter to see the tomb. It was not necessary — would not have been necessary — had I but remembered...

Our journey took us out of the Damascus Gate, northward along the road and up the hill again. As we reached the top, there still stood the three crosses, though they are empty now. I paused for a moment and relived those brief minutes of three days ago upon the hilltop.

Suddenly it was as though a clearing wind blew through me; an instant and compelling certainty enveloped me. *I remembered what the prisoner had said.*

As we stood there amidst the crowd, Jesus had looked at me and I had felt a sense of comradeship, complete comradeship, and with it the strange certainty that I belonged to him. And then he had said, "God has blessed you for this."

Of course. The thing was finished. God *had* blessed me by giving me his light, only I had not understood. No one had yet explained it to me.

That walk up the hill... This man, this prisoner, had taken me for his own during it; he had captured my love and all of my hopes — for his own. This is why I had caught the comradely warmth in his eye; without knowing it, I had been tuned to catch it.

This thing he was about to endure, this cross, had reference to me; we were comrades...and the sense of belonging — of course: I did belong to him.

I understood now.

"God has blessed you for this..." I told Peter about it as we continued our walk. There was no need for explanation; it was familiar and evident to him.

Miriam, there is no more to say about it, and yet there is so much to say, to be felt, to be enjoyed, to be attempted, to be learned. The planting is over; now comes the growth, and one day the harvest.

My dear, will I be able to share this strange beauty with you? Knowing you, I believe that I shall... And our sons, Rufus and Alexander. Our Master shall be their Master if we'll have it so.

You see, my inner strife and conflict weren't necessary. He had given himself to me and had taken me for his during our walk up the hill road, just as he has with others whom I'm meeting daily.

It is only ours to understand, and how needlessly we struggle. My love to you.

Simon.

Chapter 3

Pilate The Proconsul

Lovely Gaul can be a strange and lonely place — if it is the scene of one's banishment. This close-in colony of the Empire is still in another and alien world for Claudia and me, though life could be pleasant enough under other circumstances in this expanding hamlet; it is called "Vienna" in the local half-Teutonic tongue.

Politically, and therefore finally, life is over for me. The grossly unfair punishment I have been accorded by the Empire I served with all my heart and mind — punishment for indiscretions never committed — is bitter beyond bearing. I have always suspected that the Caesar himself, crusty old Tiberias, saw to it that I was assigned that most troublous of our lesser colonies, Judea of Palestine.

I shall never be sure of this. What is sure is that somewhere, during the years of my growing political recognition, I offended...

Claudia will be safely taken care of after I have put an end to the wearying misery of this banishment. Life under some terms is pointless... Mine is of little value now.

It is strange that out of my whole career in the service of Rome, one event should stand out with such clarity that it overshadows all else. It is worth outlining here — at the conclusion I plan for my personal life-story — because it had at the time and has had since a peculiar effect upon me. I met a man once...

He stood in my private audience chamber, alone with me. I had brought him away from a howling, brutal mob just outside so that I could better handle the strange and strong impression he had made on me just moments before, in public. Here, in private, before he spoke to me or I to him, I had the peculiar feeling that he knew me completely — knew all that there was to know about me. So strongly did this communicate that I stopped myself in some embarrassment in the unconscious act of pulling my robe more closely about me.

Stranger still was what followed immediately: suddenly I saw myself. All of the usual protective hypocrisies fell away... It was a shocking, and then numbing, experience.

Let me tell you about it in more detail. I think you will find it an unique story...

My early beginnings are not important to what I have to relate to you. My family is of Samnite extraction, as you could gather from my given name, "Pontius." My cognomen "Pilatus" is simply one I took during my younger days as a warrior in the Roman armies farther northwest of here in Gaul; my family for generations had been a warrior clan, and the name seemed to fit — or so I thought at the time.

The road of political adventure which finally led to my assignment as the 5th Procurator of Judea is too involved to concern us here, other than to note one meritorious custom that had emerged through experience and the insight of our illustrious Augustus, glory to his name: it had become the approved practice for the wives of provincial governors to accompany them to their appointed posts. Thus it was that Claudia was with me as I took ship for the port of Caesarea on the northern Judean coast.

I need to say that Claudia has stood with me in my fall as she was with me during my rise to power. Surely the one supreme act of wisdom of my career of service to the Empire was my choice of Claudia. She has been my mainstay, always. In fact, her instinct was correct on one very crucial occasion connected with the particular incident I relate here — and, may the gods forgive me, I failed finally to follow through on her cue...

I never succeeded in fully coming to understand the people of this odd land of Judea. I mention this because it has much to do with all that transpired later. At the time, I felt them to be superstitious, stubborn, and very obstinate in the face of anything Roman. They place so much — too much — faith in their accursed priests and temple authorities... I still, to this day, mistrust these worthies, although the intervening years have mellowed my judgment of them. The same could not be said, I am sure, of their feeling toward me.

Picture to yourself the feelings of Claudia and myself upon our arrival in Caesarea, when having girded ourselves for a reception at least due my station in life and government, we were keenly ignored...

I was blissfully unaware of one far-reaching fact: I was the fifth in a series of Roman Procurators each of whom had been unpopular with an enthusiastic abhorrence which can be bestowed only by a seething people whose ill will is a mix of misplaced nationalism and an almost ferocious religious fanaticism. In a word, they made it a point to have no use for their Roman governors.

As we disembarked from the ship, the wharf was innocent of anything resembling so much as a welcoming committee. Except for the baggage handlers and the harbor hirelings, my arrival had been pointedly ignored.

I summoned what dignity I could muster in the face of this hostility and proceeded with my retinue to the governor's palace, which would be our official residence for the next eight years. It was a decent enough place, hardly redolent of the grandeur of Rome but still a shining jewel in the midst of the squalor of the rest of the city of Caesarea. It had long since become the custom for the chief emissary of Rome to forego any sort of residence in the capital — the holy city of Jerusalem — other than on occasional visits. To do otherwise would have invited civic mayhem.

On our arrival in the Caesarea palace, we made ourselves comfortable and set about planning for our official visit to the capital a bit later on; this is a routine practice which is demanded of all newly appointed governors to Judea.

On the strength of the cool reception we had experienced, I decided to send two platoons of soldiers several days ahead of me to the capital; Jerusalem lay an easy three days journey to the south and east of Caesarea and at sufficient altitude in the southern mountains to insure a pleasant climate most of the year. I quietly cautioned the men of my advance guard against enjoying themselves too much prior to our arrival...

I also directed that they go fully equipped, with the silver eagles and other symbols of empire carried before them.

I caught a smile or two at this order of mine among the older soldiers who had been there, some of them, for several years. They obeyed, however, without comment. In retrospect, it is clear that I ought to have scented trouble. I felt at the time that I was following the procedure that any newly constituted emmisary of Rome would have followed.

It was four days later that I awoke in the morning to the sounds of a fearful uproar outside. I went to the window. My palace was completely surrounded by a moaning, babbling horde of these native Jews, prostrating themselves on the ground, throwing their arms in the air, gesticulating, and generally creating cacophony. My palace guard was painfully incompetent to handle the situation.

I robed quickly and hurried forth upon my upper balcony. In as authoritative a tone as I could muster in that freshly awakened and unbreakfasted hour, I ordered that the people disperse. Immediately the tumult ceased, though nobody moved. A spokesman stood forth and demanded, politely but haughtily, that the profane images which were desecrating their "holy city," as he called it, at once be removed. It took me some moments to realize that the man was referring to the insignia of empire which I had sent off to Jerusalem with the advance platoons of several days earlier.

I summarily refused his request and commanded again that the crowd disperse. Then I turned my back on them and went inside.

You will find it hard to believe that far from dispersing, the crowd resumed its din all over again. By mid afternoon the mob — and the noise — were still there. I ignored them. All night long the clamor continued outside the palace. The next day the rabble was still there — and the next.

By the sixth day of this unique performance, I felt that some demonstration of clear authority was warranted. I sent a detachment of soldiers among them and then I informed them from the balcony that if they did not desist, I would order the soldiers to begin an indiscriminate massacre. Unbelievably, these hateful people promptly laid down upon the ground and bared their necks, crying that death was preferable to the desecration of their sacred city.

Staring at them, I realized that I could not risk the matter further. Rome is not patient with its representatives who misuse power. I admit to some nervousness at this point... I acquiesced to the mob's demand with such grace as I could muster, and ordered the offending symbols removed from Jerusalem.

I relate this first incident in some detail — I could have chosen any one of a number like it — because it is a clear and classic instance of the mood and manner of this Judean populace as I experienced it. The affair hardly made me love this people I had been sent to rule in the name of Rome.

My position was difficult. I held the power of life and death over them, but the people had an uncanny way — born of long practice with my predecessors — of knowing when they were safe in defying me. I had to keep Rome as the backdrop of my planning and acting at all times — this and the figure of crusty, dyspeptic Tiberias Caesar, who was particularly touchy in these days on the point of keeping masses of people quiet and more or less content.

As I have indicated, this first incident set the pattern for several more that were to follow. Each one increased my puzzled dislike of this strange, stubborn, superstitious, treacherous people who would never really admit that Rome was its master... All that I sincerely longed to do, as the emissary of the Caesar, was to bring the people a higher culture and a more cultivated civilization, but they would have none of it — and as little of me as possible.

Our residence in Caesaria became a subtle target for the expression of the common distaste for Rome. After the first year, as much with Claudia in mind as my own inner content, we settled in delightful Caesaria Philippi, near the headwaters of the Jordan River and at the base of lovely Mount Hermon. The population here is what the Judeans would call, with disapproval, heavily Gentile. Claudia was particularly happy in this situation, and there was little talk of, and no demonstrations concerning, the Hebrew sensitivities.

As I have remarked, the usual dwelling for the Roman Proconsul was in the other Caesarea on the coast to the west. Annually I spent some weeks there pro-forma, but Caesaria Philippi was our real and delightful home for the rest of our days in the land, despite some ill-hidden disapproval on the part of Judean officialdom.

During the years that followed — almost eight of them — there were other misunderstandings. An example: I built for the capital city a new aqueduct, sorely needed, to carry water into the parched city from the Pools of Solomon, several furlongs to the south. Part of the funds to meet its cost I took from the temple treasury. This seemed only just to me — the citizenry thus helping to pay for such a public facility.

I should have expected the result: immediately I had the people about my ears, shouting imprecations and calling down upon my head the wrath of their god — one "Yahweh." My unacceptable misdeed, apparently, was that I had used what they termed sacred money to build the profane public structure. By this time, I had come to recognize familiar signs: the people had been incited to loud revolt by the temple priests who had been forced to a more modest level of living by my conscription of some of their lush funds.

On still another occasion, a formal letter of complaint went to Tiberias himself on the occasion of my decorating the residence I occupied on my brief visits to the capital: I had hung on the walls some gilt shields with the likeness of the Emporer in bas-relief. Hotly, he ordered me to remove them and I was sent a reprimand — despite the obvious fact that I had hung them in his honor. It seemed that this superstitious rabble had it written into their sacred code of laws that their Yahweh could not abide an image or a statue of any sort.

So it went, as one year melded into another. My power over them: absolute, until they went muling to Rome with their complaints...

I mentioned at the outset one incident among them all that stands out in my memory. In fact, it has never left me alone... I have never understood it, nor have I understood its strange effect upon me even down the years.

That I should have been angered to the extreme of endurance will be understandable enough as I tell the story. That I should have been forever after victimized, however, by a sense of my own paltriness and unworthiness, that I should ever since have been plagued by an odd feeling of indebtedness to a nameless power that is as far above the Emporer as the sky is above the earth — this seems almost an insanity.

Perhaps I am truly out of my mind, for it has been borne in upon me, distinctly and unmistakably, that once in my life I was in the presence of a being whose power over death — and therefore over life — was real and complete.

I am quite aware of how unlikely this seems. Perhaps it is true that my mind has been affected by my sojourn among these Hebrews with their endless pratings about their Yahweh and their heaven and their sheol.

However — on with the story of it.

In the seventh of our years in Judea, Claudia and I had gone up to Jerusalem to spend the week leading up to the annual great day for these Jews. They call it their feast of the "Passover," referring to an obscure event in early Hebrew history. I felt it necessary always to be on hand for this celebration: in the midst of their high-spirited revellings, the people tended to forget their Roman masters. I had detailed extra platoons of the palace guard to street duty during these days, as was my custom.

The feast-day fell on the Hebrew "sixth day of the week." The evening preceding, Claudia and I were in our formal room enjoying a fire in the fireplace. We always occupied the rather modest palace of Herod, the puppet king of a small northern colony called Galilee, during Passover week. I did not care for the man, nor he for me, but it had evolved into a necessity of protocol that he act the host on this annual occasion.

As Claudia and I sat enjoying the warmth and each other, there was a knock on the door. A servant announced one Caiaphus, the high priest of the colony's only temple, situated, of course, in the capital. At other places across the land were situated lesser local houses of worship called in their difficult tongue "synagogues."

At the announcement, in some despair I caught Claudia's eye. Here at our door was as surly and renegade a character as I had run across in Judea. His position rested upon his appointment by my predecessor, Valerius — with what legality in the eyes of the people I am unsure. The action was apparently taken because he was the son-in-law of an aged priest of high standing by the name of Annas — from whom, it was rumored, the high priest had learned his devious ways.

Caiaphus was a cunning and avaricious man. On entering our room on this occasion, he cleared his throat... There was a man, he said, who was dangerous to the public welfare; Caiaphus's coterie wanted this man put out of the way. This was the gist of a rambling and obsequious recital. I asked the name of the man and his crime; Caiaphus mumbled into his ridiculous beard and coughed delicately.

When I asked where the man was at the moment, the priest muttered that he would be delivered to my presence on the morrow. He added that he would personally appreciate a speedy trial and conviction — and peered at me glitteringly... I knew what this brute in robes meant. The wooden cross which we Romans had introduced was being used here too frequently of late as a means of common execution: these officials regarded it as edifying to the populace in that presumably it discouraged lawbreaking.

I could stand no more of Caiaphus and rose to my feet. He bowed with insinuating slowness and retired.

It was then that I noticed Claudia's nervousness.

"I believe I know of the man the priest refers to," she said. "Pontius, he is no lawbreaker and no seditionist. He has merely been teaching the people publicly, and — so I have heard repeatedly — healing some of them who suffer illness. The priestly faction has been fearful of his growing power with the people."

She laid her hand on my arm. "Surely, Rome's ideal of justice precedes petty local considerations."

I listened to her then... Would that I had listened and acted in accordance with her plea on a later occasion...

Too early the next morning, I was awakened and routed out of bed by the news of a mob descending upon me. I let them cool their heels in my audience hall while I dressed slowly, and then went to sit before them on my throne. It was an illegal hour according to Roman colonial law, but I had learned to expect the worst in Passover week.

This proved to be a noisy group, a number of temple figures among them, and they all began to talk at once the moment I appeared. The only silent one among them was a prisoner they had, a quiet looking chap; in other circumstances, you might not have noticed him in a gathering of people — not, that is, until he looked at you. His eyes, without being piercing or accusative, yet held you in a sort of quiet assessment. I don't know how else to describe his presence... His hands were bound in front of him with thongs, and they were leading him by a cord tied loosely about his waist.

The leaders of the lot had apparently remained outside; their excuse for this would have been their fear of polluting themselves by entering the house of a non-Jew on their high holy day, and thus being unable to partake of their feast that evening. Here was more of their childish superstition.

I went out to my porch to discover a large crowd, peppered with religious dignitaries, on the terrace beyond. I held up my hand for silence.

"What accusation do you bring against this man?" I asked them.

It appeared that my question took them by surprise. Evidently, Caiaphus had assured them that all was well and that I would sentence the prisoner at once without interrogation.

My anger grew. For quite personal reasons, I became more determined than before to free the prisoner.

No answer to my question was forthcoming until one surly old fellow mumbled, "If he were not a malefactor, we would not have delivered him up to you."

This was no answer to my inquiry... I determined to teach them a lesson.

"Very well," I said, allowing the contempt I felt for them full reign as I spoke. "Take him and judge him according to your law." This was an unwelcome thrust. As subjects of Rome, local authorities had no right of capital conviction; in this place, I and I alone could impose the death sentence.

My refusal to act against their prisoner threw the throng into paroxysms of helpless anger. They milled about in discontent; shouts of blame and accusation against their prisoner grew louder. There had rather clearly been a rehearsal for this scene... The man was accused of perverting the nation, of forbidding his hearers to pay tribute, of calling himself a king.

I turned my back on the crowd and returned to the audience hall. There, I beckoned the prisoner to come alone with me into my private judgement chamber. The man interested me. It was obvious upon simply an initial glance at him that he was neither a rabble-rouser nor a rascal.

I sat down — it was early and I had had no breakfast — and I looked up at the figure standing before me. He was dressed in the ordinary seamless under-robe of his countrymen; his outer robe and sash had been taken from him at some point.

There was nothing ordinary, however, about his face. He was relaxed, and he was looking at me without either fear or hostility. Those eyes, though, quite suddenly made me uncomfortable. Difficult as it is to believe, for a moment I felt as though I were the accused, and he the judge.

He looked worn, as though he had been allowed little sleep, and he was tousled. The Jewish authorities had not been handling him kindly. To my dying day, though, I will never forget what I can only call the kingly bearing of him: not haughty — simply regal, in the purest sense. It is both strange and disconcerting to have the memory of him stay with me as it has — and does to this moment.

I cleared my throat.

"Are you indeed the king of the Jews?" I asked. As I put the question, I had meant to sound quietly disdainful — the ruling Roman addressing a colonial. To my surprise, I heard myself asking an honest question: I wanted to know...

He looked at me with dignity, a gentle sort of dignity. Those eyes... This is when I caught myself pulling my robe more closely about me. I felt unconsciously as though he were looking through me, into me.

Then he spoke. "Do you ask this of yourself, or did others tell it to you about me?"

He was adroit — answering my question with his own question. He admitted nothing, and he put me into a defensive posture. In spite of myself, I smiled. Amazingly, he smiled too, with that quiet dignity of his.

I strove to recover command of the conversation.

"Am I a Jew?" I asked. "Your own nation, even your chief priests, have delivered you to me. What have you done?"

He reverted then to my first question.

"My kingdom is not of this world. If it were, then my servants would fight."

I wrestled for a moment with the implications of this, and then I looked at him narrowly. Was he going so far as to joke with me? What sort of fighting force could a man like this have at his command?

Then I saw that he was deadly serious. His kingdom — not of this world... Whatever odd thing he had in mind, he was sincere: he had meant what he said.

I spoke again, trying to interpret. "Are you a king then?"

It was as though he had been waiting for this question. His eyes had never left my face, and now, as I looked back at him, I felt the full force of them

"You say that I am a king," he answered. "To this end have I been born and to this end have I come into the world that I should bear witness to the truth."

The truth... Hardest of all entities to catch. In my earlier days in Rome, over good glasses of wine through long evenings, my friends and I would argue endlessly over the nature of truth; it had been the fashion at the time.

The truth... I started to do something, and then I stopped myself: I've been particularly sorry for this, because since that fateful morning, I've come to feel that this might have been the key, and unwittingly, I rejected it. What I had intended in that lost moment was to ask him what he meant, what this truth of his was...

Then, accursedly, my pride and my Roman persona intruded. I had best be done with the matter... I retreated to the old philosophical question redolent of long evenings in officers quarters.

"What is truth?" I asked — cynically, I'm afraid intending an end to the conversation.

The effect of my words almost frightened me. The man's face changed expression: it saddened, quite as though I had closed a door against him physically... Never will I forget that silent mutation.

Beyond doubting, however, the man had won me.

I rose quickly, strode forth into the audience hall, through the rabble and onto the porch, leaving the prisoner alone in the judgement room. I held up my hand for silence, and without preamble I gave my decree of acquittal.

"I find in him no fault at all."

After a few moments of stunned silence, the storm broke — a flood of shouted protest. Those inside heard, and came pouring forth to join their leaders. Among other accusations, one that caught my attention was that the prisoner was a "meshith," a disturber, having upset the people all the way from Galilee to here with his teachings.

The man, then, was a Galilean — and thus it was that I made my fatal mistake. How different the ending would have been had I remained firm in my first decision. As so frequently before, I found the shouting frightening. Suddenly I was afraid — afraid of Caiaphus, afraid of this violent, rehearsed mob, afraid of the twisted word that might filter back to Rome.

I was not yet ready to convict, but perhaps I could evade the issue... I directed that the man be taken before Herod, the Galilean Tetrarch: let him sentence the man to some suitable minor punishment.

The leaders of the mob did not care for the idea, but surlily they agreed: I knew that they saw in this the possibility of accomplishing their purpose... So it was that the prisoner was led off across the city, and so it was that peace reigned once again in the hot morning sun about my palace.

What I should have recognized is that one evasion would lead to another: unerringly, it does. At the moment, however, I had been confused, headstrong and not a little angry; I craved to be rid of the whole politically charged situation.

It was hardly two hours before I heard the mob as it returned across the city. My heart sank, and I went again to my throne on the porch.

Would that I could blot out the memory of that next hour...

My first evasion was my fatal one, for it weakened my position critically. Caiaphus had done his work well: this rehearsed throng was determined to have its prisoner executed. Nothing less would do.

Herod had simply returned the prisoner to me; there were no remarks, suggestions or recommendations. The man was back on my hands, literally for life or death.

Struggling for an answer I could live with, I decided to try a half-way course. I told the crowd that I would scourge the prisoner, by way of punishment, and then I would set him free... This scourge, as it is practiced in Judea, is frightening; the whips are frequently garnished with knots and bits of broken metal.

I should say that I had made one attempt to free the man even before this point had been reached. It was the traditional custom on this feast day to choose one criminal, in prison for serious crime, and set him free. I had held my hand up for quiet, demanded an hour's time to consider the matter, and sent word to the head jailer of Jerusalem's city prison.

The man the jailer sent, not a choice I would have made, was a somewhat popular rebel against Roman authority — a frequent offender by the name of Barabbas. Less than wisely, however, I followed through on my plan to have the crowd render judgement between the two prisoners. In all honesty, I had been so won by the Galilean prisoner that I failed to see how the unkempt Barabbas could be preferred.

As I was setting the matter forth before the crowd, a slave hurried across the platform; he bore a tablet and, bowing, he handed it to me. In the wax was a brief note from Claudia: "Have nothing to do with this just man, for I have suffered many things this day in a dream because of him."

The note fed me courage. Almost, I stood and commanded on pain of death that the crowd disperse and the prisoner Jesus of Nazareth be set free... Almost...

In a moment of hesitation, my fears, my despicable fears, once again descended upon me. Caiaphus, the power of the other temple authorities, their friends in Rome...

In my quick agony, my eyes sought the man from Nazareth. He was ignoring the crowd and looking at me. Our eyes met. I can remember to this moment his effect on me: it was as though he were pouring strength into me... I started to my feet.

Then — once again, came my fears — my contemptible, craven fears. I closed my eyes and looked away — a moment of indecision that was my final undoing.

It was in this brief span of time that the temple leaders had passed the word to the uncertain crowd that it was to call for Barabbas. This the people did, at the top of their rough and hoarse voices.

I had lost the battle, and I knew it then. I grasped at one last straw to make the crowd reverse its decision: perhaps if the responsibility for punishment were on the people...

"What do you want me to do with the King of the Jews then?" I cried.

Then came, for the first time, the mad scream; it was started by just a handful of men in one corner but it was quickly taken up by a mob that was now near the point of hysteria: "Crucify him! Crucify him!"

In vain, I tried to protest, shouting into their pauses for breath...

"Why? What evil has he done?"

"I find no cause for death in him."

"I will chastise him and let him go."

So I shouted — and was repeatedly shouted down... "Crucify! Crucify him!"

There was no way out for me — no way. I had lost it with my first evasion... I set Barabbas free and turned the Galilean over to a squad of my soldiers. They were gone for most of an hour, during which interval I went inside and paced the hall while the mob remained outside, pushing and jostling.

I returned to my seat on the porch as they brought the man forth. There was a gasp from the crowd, and a few rougher ones laughed. They had half-killed the poor fellow: there was blood all over his body from the knotted whips. More, they had ridiculed his kingly pretensions by weaving a mock crown out of some thorn branches from the garden; blood was running on his forehead.

My moment of hope that the shocked throng had seen enough was soon dashed.

I stood. "Behold the man!" I cried, half expecting to hear cries of "Enough! Free him!"

There were a few moments of silence. I held my breath.

Then, a single shout on this side, answered on that and quickly taken up from all sides — "On with it! Crucify him!"

Just once more I tried to shout into the crowd, and it was as a drop of water thrown against a waterfall, as my subtly pursuing fear whispered the danger of Rome...

I was afraid to look again at the prisoner; I had the feeling that I would catch his eye... Quickly I called for a bowl of water, to enact before them their ancient Judean symbol. I dipped my hands and spoke into the sudden silence.

"You take him and crucify him, for I find no fault in him!"

They led him away. I did not see him again.

Justice?

There was surely none of it here. I was afraid — with the old Roman fear of political extinction.

I told myself over and over again in the days that followed that it had all been for the good cause of colonial quiet and appeasement — that one mere Galilean life was not too great a price to pay for civic peace.

Yet — that man. He keeps coming back — in moments of unshielded thought, even in my nightly dreaming. With him comes the sting of my own cowardice: I did him to death...

With the thought, or memory — or presence — of this man comes the reminder of the lack of honor, the denial of justice, which was the final path I chose. It is as though these things are slowly being burnt, cleansed away from within me: I can't experience it any other way or call it by any other name.

His kingdom, he said, was not of this world. I have come to believe that he did have a kingdom. I wonder where it was. More, I wonder how the truth of which he spoke took shape. I have wished with all my heart that I had let him tell me that day when we were alone in the judgement hall. I think he was about to do so.

He is gone. Few are yet alive who knew him, and when they are gone, any memory of him will die with them. Then, none shall ever hear of him again.

Because of me — none shall ever hear of him again.

Chapter 4

The Rock

He was sitting on a smooth natural ledge overhanging the water, and he saw that I was a strolling stranger. We fell easily and naturally into conversation, and when he mentioned the Galilean, I sat down near him on his rocky ledge and encouraged him to speak further.

What he had to say captured my interest quickly. In my career as a clerk, I had noticed in several of my Sanhedrin clients a negatory interest in this condemned Nazarene, executed several months ago, that was more pronounced than was usual in such cases.

Apparently, my new acquaintance had known the man rather intimately: just how intimately I wasn't at first prepared to accept... I also found myself skeptical of some of the claims concerning the Galilean that I was hearing here for the first time. I'm afraid my hesitation showed...

We sat that day for a long while in conversation. I record here what I can accurately recall of what my new acquaintance had to say.

You ask me why I'm sure — so sure of him. This may be difficult for me to answer... That the man was the Messiah for whom the Hebrew people have so long waited, that he was uniquely God's messenger, that he has the power to replace a person's selfish will with his own will — these things are no longer mere possibilities with me. They are facts, firm and stark, and real beyond any reality I have known.

One day, I believe, many people, even as far away as Rome and beyond, will understand what and who he was — and is. Right now, however, it is all a new thing for people to grasp.

Perhaps it will help if I tell you something of my experience of him. Simply my life with him was not enough; I wasn't sure of him until that...cross.

Capernaum here has been my home for as long as my memory reaches. As you've seen, it's a lovely town, alongside its beautiful lake. I suppose *you* would call it a village, used as you are to Jerusalem with all of its big-city focus.

Capernaum has always been enough for me. Its streets are quiet and clean; a man can think as he walks, and its homes are filled with content. Our primary industry, I suppose, is our fishing, though there are vineyards about, too, and fields — some of them rising a third of the way up the foot-slopes of our surrounding hills.

We sons of Jonah had been raised on fishing — and we did well. I think it is only the truth for me to say that I was a different sort of fellow in those days. Being sure of myself and loving my work and being a bit proud of my business prowess, I established myself only a few years beyond youth as the leading fisher of the town. At twenty-one, I was an employer — of several men. One of them was my older brother Andrew; I held him in just a shade of affectionate disdain for what I considered his lack of enterprise...

I owned three boats by this time, and I made a point of keeping the best and neatest fleet on the sea — our little Sea of Galilee here. Some call it simply a lake. I painted the boats yellow; the fleet of Simon bar-Jonah was a town institution.

Three times a week I trudged up the hill over there that is graced by the formidable winter palace of Herod Antipas himself. We still today put up with him, having little choice... But it was a point of considerable pride with me in those heady days to serve the palace personally as its appointed fisher.

When you put it all together, I was proud of my boats and proud of my success and proud of my place in the community — in fact, I was proud of myself.

Then — my pleasant, proud world was turned upside down and shattered...

I couldn't see it coming; how could I have been expected to?

I had little use for gentle people; I failed to understand the strength that is in gentleness: and how gentle he was... It is strange that I should have been so captivated.

It was natural that my gentle brother Andrew should have been the first to notice the visitor's subtle power — Andrew and young John, who had come across the fellow one day when they were on an afternoon jaunt together. He had recently come to Capernaum from his native Nazareth in the large valley to the west of us. I'm not sure why; I suppose he liked being near the shore.

He had no home, and he was sleeping in his succoth — the small wattled booth you've seen hereabout, used by us Galileans when we're on pilgrimage or any extended trip; he had thrown a cloak over the top for a roof.

It seemed that Andrew and John had discovered him there and had held a long conversation with him; they were gone all of one night — they may have slept near him, for all we knew.

The next morning they came down to the boats with a queer manner about them. We were scheduled to spend the day on the water, but they informed me that they weren't fishing that day, and that what was more, I wasn't either because I was coming with them to meet — Jesus...

I suppose I must have gaped in amazement. Neither of them had ever before told *me* what to do... Then they turned on their heels and Andrew repeated over his shoulder that I was to come with them. I suppose I was surprised into obedience: it was a new experience for me... Meekly, I went with them.

The man Jesus, this Nazarene, was sitting on a stone beside his small shelter on the outskirts of town... It was as though he had been waiting for us; perhaps he had been... I don't know what John and Andrew had told him, but quietly he watched us as we walked toward him.

On our arrival at his side, he smiled and motioned to us to sit down. Andrew and John were too engrossed in him to introduce me, but this didn't matter because he knew my name...

His personality had a strange effect; I've tried to describe this before: he made the world close about us seem better than we knew it really was. I can't explain this in detail; it was a *presence* that he had, if you can grasp that.

We chatted awhile. I had never before experienced anyone so magnetic; so effortlessly it was that he held people to him...

Finally, he turned to me. The full force of that magnetism was almost overwhelming as he spoke.

"Simon," he said, "you're a fisher. I'm sure you're a good one."

I remember his words because, true to form, my chest began to swell — and then I caught the undertone of quiet amusement in his voice. It was very slight, but it was enough... I flushed.

Then the amusement was gone. Without preamble, he said to me, "I have a task to perform. I think you could help me... Will you leave your boats and come with me?"

There it was: no explanation, no promises, no sharing of his plans. It was completely without reason or sense — and the most amazing thing of all was that I caught myself about to say, "Yes, of course..."

I choked back the words, aware that I had to escape this dangerous magnetism of his. I leapt to my feet and strode hurriedly away, afraid to trust myself to say anything... I had to get back to reality, to my boats. The man's request was unthinkable and — well — absurd.

I busied myself for the rest of the day with odd tasks among the nets and the rigging. I didn't see Andrew or John again until nightfall. Well after the dinner hour, Andrew came to the beach and saw me on the *Esther*, our large boat, where it bobbed softly at anchor. He called to me and I told him to take word back that I would be home directly.

In fact, I didn't go home — not all that night. I remember only vaguely those passing hours as I sat on the stern and gazed vacantly out over the far reaches of water... My life was so ordered, so planned out... I was doing so nicely — and then this — this odd fellow with his nonsensical talk...

I laughed at myself — and then faced the fact that my laughing was humorless... None of it made sense — and yet I was wrestling, wrestling hard. But — with what? What was it?

My boats, my lovely boats. I glanced about in the warm moonlight. Yes, there they were, all three: the little *Naomi*, so fleet and slender; the *Ruth*, our sturdy barge — and my beloved *Esther*. Leave them?

By morning, I had taken refuge once again in my old, familiar bravado. I felt ready to face Andrew and John now, and to face them down. I rowed myself to the beach and fell to work on our large net; we were replacing cracked floats. The other fellows would be down soon.

A shadow fell across the net; here was one of them now. I stood and turned to face — him. It wasn't Andrew or John: it was this fellow Jesus...

The early morning sun was slanting across the water and the sand, and as he looked at me, I felt all my pride and certainty slipping away. I felt somehow naked and empty.

He looked down. "Those are very good nets," he said. "Fish would have a hard time slipping through them."

Then — "Simon, I would like to make you a fisher of men... Will you come with me?"

A fisher — of men? My lovely boats, my life and the comforts I had earned; my reputation in the town. All of these good things... Lose them? And — for what?

I started to speak. "I don't think I..."

He was still looking down. I know now that he didn't intend to help me; this was to be my decision... No sense to it. It was completely alien to my well-ordered thinking, my well-planned life.

...Suddenly I said, "Yes, I'll come" — and I knew immediately that the wrestling was over. I didn't know whether I had won or lost but the wrestling was over, and there was a feeling, first, of vast relief.

I stood waiting for the blow that I was sure would come: the reaction, the sudden, deep sense of loss — my boats, all the things of value to which I had given my life.

The blow did not come, because now he helped me. He looked up at me and smiled, warmly and intimately. That magnetism!

I suppose he saw the tenseness in my eyes, the waiting... He looked out across the water at the boats once, fleetingly.

"You won't miss them, Simon," he said and then he started to walk along the beach, and I followed him. I have thought about it often since. I don't think I looked back...

It was easy to find my place in the Master's scheme of things. If there were difficult adjustments to make, I have little recollection of them now.

Perhaps because I was a bit taller and physically stronger than some of the others, I found myself adopting the role of foreman when he preached to the people on the hillsides of Galilee or in the villages. First there were groups of people that gathered; later there were crowds. They would be tractable enough until he began to heal some who were ill or suffering. Then, as was only too natural, the people would try to jamb and force their way to him. I found it expedient at times to exert my authority and to make them form neat lines and take their proper turns...

In honesty, I must add that authority and I were often poor bedfellows. It was so easy for me to make of these healings an end in themselves, rather than one means to the higher end Jesus had in view.

It was surprising enough that these restorations to health were worked through him. There was surely nothing "magical" about it, however. Our bodies are the servants of our minds and our emotions, not the masters of them. One who was in touch intuitively with God, as Jesus surely was, is therefore also in touch intuitively with something of divine power over the body and its illnesses. Jesus was never the creator here: he was simply the channel.

It followed, as I slowly learned, that the Master could heal effectively only where there was an almost complete surrender to him, a surrender which involved both the mind and the heart... I came to recognize that he was forced to discover in each supplicant whether there indeed was this complete surrender to the presence and the power and the love of God as these were operative through him.

There was the constant threat of tragedy — the tragedy of those from whom the Master was forced to turn away...

(Here my brawny friend paused; he seemed to slip easily into protracted periods of silence and, I suppose, remembering. I had learned by now simply to wait without interrupting... A bird moved in some shore reeds nearby and a breeze riffled the green shallows and then moved outward toward the blue depths. Finally, as I knew he would, he spoke again. His story had only begun.)

People have missed the mark when they've assumed that Jesus was all-powerful... I have come to realize in these latter days that he was not all-powerful. He was limited as God is limited — to those who were dead to everything except his intuitive divinity, God's living presence through him. There could be no compromise, no half-giving of a heart, no careful reservations. I know, because I tried each of these subterfuges myself...

This necessary first searching of each supplicant, as the long lines of the suffering presented themselves, was an exhausting burden for the Master. I have seen him nearly dead with fatigue after a few hours of it. Gradually he allowed me to assume the right to call a halt for a few hours or for a day, while he went apart, usually alone, to refresh and renew himself. I learned from him how far I could go in this, and in the process I learned much about curbing and commanding myself.

For a long while, there were rarely any who would speak a word of ridicule against him — including the disappointed ones whom he might not heal. Even his enemies — and he began to have them in high places because he spoke the unflinching truth — even these hesitated to call him an imposter or a charlatan.

I suppose it was the Master's magnetism; I've indicated to you already how this cast the shape of my life... When you knew him even superficially, you found yourself expecting him to do amazing things. It would then have seemed strange if he had *not* made use of the divine powers being channeled through him.

It remains the odd fact that none called Jesus a deceiver — not, that is, until near the end, when he began to speak openly of his great design and his deeper identity. More and more, he adopted the manner and the words and the symbols of the Messiah, the traditional figure, as you are aware, who is to save Israel from her conquerors. His design was for far more than this: it encompassed the world — all peoples everywhere and for all time.

However, as all of Jerusalem now knows, it was at this point that Jesus touched the defensive sensitivity of many in our local populace and of *all* the temple authorities. As he consciously and purposely wove about himself signs and symbols of Messiahship, his enemies were given a weapon to use against him; all of us close to him sensed that if he persisted along the path he had chosen, they would not spare him for long.

I've always been glad that he knew of my complete surrender to him... I had long known that he was great, somehow uniquely powerful among us. I knew that he was not like other men: he was my Master and I completely his servant.

However, it required a point-blank question he directed to me one day to prove that — let me state it simply — that for me, he was God's son in a complete and final way.

We were on our way north, some days before he led us, much against our wills, down to Jerusalem. We had left Bethsaida Julius and were on our way to Caesaria Phillipi, north of our Sea... We had been walking for some hours; it was a lovely day for travelling, I remember, with just a slight haze over a bright sun and air that was crisp and still... We were alone, too; it was a relief to be for a blessed while away from the crowds.

As we walked, however, it was clear that something was troubling the Master. He was never shallowly talkative, but he was always a good companion. On this day he walked as one alone, with much on his mind.

At mid-morning he called a halt, and told us to wait by the road. He walked off at an angle into a small green canyon and was alone — in prayer, I suppose — for most of an hour... This was not unusual.

Then he returned, seeming a bit less tense, and we resumed our journey. It was then, as we walked, that he asked us his strange first question.

"Who do men say that I, the Son of Man, am?" It was a phrase, a title, that the Master used with reference to himself frequently; none of us were quite sure what he meant by it. I came gradually to believe that he looked upon himself as belonging, literally, to all people. He cared nothing for property or for position. The summit of his longing was to *give* himself — to become the possession of his fellows... It is difficult to put this sort of thing into words: this is about as close as I can come to it.

The question that he asked — "Who do people say that I am?" — was a difficult one for us, not because we had no answer, but because we knew that all the answers we could give him were the wrong ones... We had picked up numerous rumors and stories being carried about on the common tongue. Some thought Jesus to be a returned prophet — Isaiah or Jeremiah. Others claimed that he was the re-embodied spirit of John the Baptizer, who had been recently beheaded by Herod. All sorts of odd conclusions emerged, most of them tied to the common ancient traditions.

Hesitantly, we shared all of this with the Master; these were the unpleasant truths, and he would have nothing but the truth.

With deep concern, I watched his face mirror his sense of failure. He had been teaching and preaching for almost three years now, and was this the end of it all — this superstition, this gross misunderstanding of what he was trying to be, to say? Was there nowhere among the people — some who were grasping after what he struggled to do — to open them to a fresh and new conception of God and therefore a new relationship with him?

I had never before felt so grieved for the Master, so completely sorry for him — no, nor even later when they took him to try him for his life. Here he was staring stark failure in the face. Perhaps nowhere had he really planted the seed of his amazing message, nowhere — not even in the hearts of —

Then it was that for the first time I knew genuine oneness with him. I sensed that for once I had been thinking utterly with him. I believe that here was my moment of greatest insight, my truest knowledge of my Master. I had known exactly what was on his mind and what he was going to ask with his next question.

He spoke it so quietly and hesitantly that only those of us nearest to him heard: "But — who do *you* say that I am?"

I believe that for a moment, he was terribly afraid. If none of us had understood, there was little hope that anyone had: his whole program and ministry — a failure...

In that moment, I looked into his inmost soul; it was perhaps the only time that I saw him clearly. In the act, I saw myself, and I knew that I was his for now and for eternity, that though I might in my weakness fail him time and again, always I would know him for who he was.

I answered him from the depths of my heart.

"You are the Christ, the Son of the living God."

To see his face clear, to see the fear and the haunting hurt be replaced by an expression of inward peace and certainty and gratitude — this was all the reward that I shall ever ask of earth or of heaven... He turned to me, his eyes so warm that my own immediately brimmed over, and he blessed me. Also, he called me "Petros," a rock, his rock, one on whom he could trust and depend. Thus, I have been called Peter; by his word, I was no longer Simon.

This incident, I believe, was the high point of my relationship with him while he was here with us in the flesh.

It was several months later that the end came, and it was upon us so suddenly that even those of us nearest to him didn't recognize its immanence beforehand.

I must admit that I had done my best to keep the Master from going to Jerusalem; all of us had done the same, except the young John... I didn't understand John at the time, but I have come to acknowledge since that he saw the whole picture more clearly than any of the rest of us. Temperamentally and mentally, he was of us all nearest to Jesus.

John saw that the course the Master had taken would end only one way. The others of us saw this also, with fear and bewilderment. But John saw farther — beyond the horizon of Jesus's coming condemnation. He knew that death would not be the end... He alone among us all held to this trust.

Thus it was that while the rest of us wept and worried, John simply waited, dry-eyed, alone and misunderstood. He sat silent, eyes upon his Master, during our Passover dinner together, the last meal we shared with Jesus.

It was only a few hours later, while the Master was praying for guidance and strength in the Garden of Gethsemane out on the Mount, that they came and took him: a dissolute mob they were, with a few soldiers among them to keep some semblance of order. Even there, I snatched up my sword, prepared to defend him. He reproved me, and I retreated with a sense of personal rejection. I didn't yet see what John had recognized long since.

Later, when the Master was on trial, I stole into the courtyard of the high priest's palace looking for information, for some way that I could manage to free him. They marked me there as being one of his disciples; my attempt was an abject failure. I had to lie my way out of the thing. The whole blunder was a terrible experience after having shared the honesty and purity of life with him.

In the trials that followed — two before Pilate, the Roman Procurator, and one before the Tetrarch, Herod — I struggled through deep frustration. Added to this, as I now know, was fear for myself, fear that I might be forced to share his fortunes...

It is idle, of course, to wish for a thing after the opportunity has forever passed, but I have longed so often since that I had had the courage to stand there at the foot of the cross, instead of far out, safely on the edge of the crowd...that in his suffering, Jesus could have seen me there as he looked down. I would give my life now — all that I shall ever be — if I could relive and reshape my part in those last mortal hours of his.

After it was over, we gathered quietly late on that awful sixth day. We were in the upper room of a friend — the same room in which we had supped with the Master the evening before. We spoke little, except for young John; he was telling us about it because he alone of us all had been there at the foot of the cross.

I need to say that John was the calmest among us. Long before the recital was over, the bitterness of our loss had taken hold of us all — all except John, as he talked to us. He merely shared his story, and then he sat quietly in his place and told us to wait — not to lose hope, but to wait.

Thus the night passed, and the next awful day.

Then it was the first day of the week... How can I lead you fully to understand what we experienced that morning?

I had been sleeping fitfully — the first sleep I had had in almost two days time. It was Mary of Magdala who aroused us not long after dawn.

The first we knew was a pounding on the door — and then she was telling us, her words pouring out in such a quick flood that it was difficult to follow her story... Mary had gone with others of the women of our company to anoint the Master's body in the tomb. They expected the rolling-stone to be sealed, and word had come that the Governor's captain had posted a guard. They were confident, however, that they would be allowed to perform this last service of love.

Mary had hurried ahead and had arrived first — to find the guard gone, the stone rolled back, and the tomb empty... The Roman soldiers, I knew, might well be punished by death for the dereliction of allowing grave robbers or vandals to disturb a guarded tomb.

It was then that I saw John on his feet, moving toward the closed door of our room: he was going to see for himself... I called to him to pause for a moment, and shortly the two of us were running full tilt through the still silent streets as the dawn grew stronger and the early rays of the sun slanted down upon us.

John, a decade my junior, reached the garden first. I found him waiting for me, surveying the scene before him intently. The soft earth was clearly trampled as by several pairs of running feet. The great disc-stone in its groove was rolled back from the mouth of the tomb, as Mary had said.

I didn't pause further. I rushed across to the opening and inside as John followed me, and as I stood gasping for breath, I found it difficult to believe my own eyes...

There on the floor of the cavern, in the growing morning light filtering in, were the linen cloths in which they had wrapped the Master's body two days before. The body itself had disappeared...

I looked at John. Was it possible? The Master had said he would rise up from death, but most of us hadn't believed him literally and actively. He had so often spoken to us in parabolic form, his meaning to be grasped in similarity and suggestion.

One of us, though, had discerned the difference here, had sensed the actuality and the promise in the Master's words, their shocking reality — one of us into whose eyes I was looking...

"I told you to wait," cried John, his face transfigured with a joy and a certainty such as I had never seen before, nor shall again.

"This is the way it had to be," he said. "Don't you see? He had to die. He had to experience and to conquer this last awful thing that frightens us all so much — in order to prove his words about his loving care for all of us, here and — yes — hereafter, about the life open to us beyond earthly time. Don't you remember what he said one day about going ahead of us, his word that 'I go to prepare a place for you'..."

...For three years I had been with the Master. I had seen him heal people's bodies — and even more central, their minds and spirits. I had seen him live life and make of it a triumph; I had heard him speak words that had shaped other lives into similar triumph — and yet this, this was hard for me. *Could* the Master have come alive from death?

John had started back already to share our findings with the others. I let him hurry ahead: one was enough to bear the news. I had to think, to savor this new thing, to find my own bearings of faith.

We were together that night, all of us and the two Marys and Martha. John had no doubts left. Others of us were slower to accept what seemed to have happened. Thomas was skeptical of the whole thing.

Then it was that he came to us...

There was no doubting his presence. He was there for each one of us, in the form that was needed for each: he was visible and tactile for the previously doubting Thomas, he spoke to those who needed to hear his voice in order to believe, and the familiar pressure of his person was strong upon all of us. It was as though he enveloped us singly and individually with his particular and personal care for us. It was a moving experience beyond description, yet strangely serene, perhaps the apex of the human story. And I — I was judged worthy to share it...

Prior to and separate from this experience, however, my decision had been made. Actually, I had known all along... The words that Jesus spoke. The life that he lived. His attitude toward his fellows. His love for all living things. His grasp of truth. His convictions concerning himself: "No man comes to the Father but by me." Imagine a human being saying that! "I, if I be lifted up, will draw all people to myself." "Come to me, all you who labor and are heavy laden, and I will give you rest." "In my Father's house are many mansions; if it were not so, I would have told you. I go to prepare a place for you."

In thinking on these things, I had already asked myself whether any person could have spoken such words and coupled with them a life of complete personal sacrifice — and been other than the son of the living God.

It was but a few of us who were privileged to share his life as I did. But it was not until the final crucial experience was reached, the ending of it all, that I knew him at last for who and what he was... Our minds move slowly, and we are stubborn creatures. Only because God is patient is there hope for any one of us.

The Master called me Peter. I am going out to be his rock — his steadfast support — to preach him to all who will listen, to preach him crucified...and risen. I am going out to share what I know.

He asked me once what I thought of him, who he was — and I told him.

"You are the Christ, the son of the living God."

Chapter 5

The Centurion

It is about the year A.D. 30. In a military prison cell in Rome a young officer, a Centurion, sits with several sheets of vellum before him. He has been motionless, in deep thought, for many minutes. At length he takes up his pen, dips, and begins to write.

I assume you are aware, your Grace, of my deep appreciation. I am familiar with the course which our military law must take, and it is a tribute to your generosity that you allow me to make an official report as an officer of the armies of Rome.

In gratitude, I shall write with complete honesty and candor. I am persuaded that such is your concern and your wish...

It was simply military contingency that assigned me to Palestine. There was not to be found a man in my legion who would have chosen to be sent there. I remember well the pronouncements the government put forth to interest some of us into volunteering. It sounded pleasant — and fooled none of us. Eventually the high command had simply to assign us; they must surely have suspected that no one would choose such a mission voluntarily.

So it was that I discovered my name on the lists one morning and was allowed only five days to make my preparations.

To my surprise, the sea voyage was a delight: this I must acknowledge. It was early summer, when the winds are favorable and gentle. Our officers' quarters were in the stern cabin section among the rooms reserved for the more wealthy civilian passengers. In the cabin next to mine, in fact, was a Jewish merchant who had been living in Rome for some years although he was a native of Judea.

This interesting man took a liking to me, and I to him. It was a strange sort of friendship, for on the surface we had nothing in common. The gentleman even took it upon himself to converse at great length with me about his religion, of all things.

My attitude at first was politely scornful. I'm sure he must have sensed this. In my career as a soldier of the Empire, I had had little time for the gods. I was not particularly hostile, I must have you understand. I simply felt that the gods could take care of themselves and were probably pretty occupied at the task; their interest in me would be very minor, and so we would preserve a politely disinterested distance.

However, this wealthy, quiet-spoken Jew had a great deal of interest in the gods, or as he took pains to have me understand, *in the only one God there is.*

It is peculiarly Jewish, your Grace, to believe in this one God. This may seem strange to you, as it did to me — at first... Now — well, let me give you the full story of all that happened to me. I shall be as succinct as a complete report will allow.

As I have said, this gracious Jewish gentleman, who had the name of Jacob — a name typical of his Hebrew culture — Jacob talked a great deal about "Yahweh," as he called him. This God is a creative and personal being; he has made the world and everything in it. More, he is a jealous God: he resents a person's worshipping anything or anyone but himself. He is constantly watching over those who put themselves at his service, and it is even possible that he will communicate his wishes to an individual person in some way and on some occasions.

This God, this Yahweh, is a very systematic being, or so thought my Jewish friend. He expects and requires that certain rules be followed, particularly on the seventh day of the week, which is the Jewish holy day. This day is called the "Sabbath."

I must say that all of this seemed a bit ridiculous to me at the time, and I am afraid that I conveyed this to Jacob as we sat together on the gently swaying deck. It *still* seems ridiculous — all of the regulations and rules, I mean — although I am by no means now prepared to ridicule Jacob's God.

The most moving thing about it to me, as we sat for hours by the low wooden railing watching the quiet waters slide by, was that my friend truly allowed this Yahweh of his to rule his life. His trust of his God was not simply a fetish, a formality for display purposes. It was more like the relationship of a Centurion to his General — or even to his Caesar. Jacob lived all the time, every moment, in the consciousness of this living being who was concerned constantly in what he, Jacob, did and said.

I have introduced you to the thinking of this man at some length, your Grace, not because he himself is important in the events which were later to occur, but because he was so typical of his people. He belonged to a group in Jewish society known as Pharisees, a religious-social upper class to whom the common people pay considerable respect. I was to meet many of his stamp later, though few with his kindliness of heart.

We landed in due course in the little city of Joppa, one of the only two seaports along the Judean coastline. It wasn't as bad as I had expected, although the heat from mid-morning to mid-afternoon was genuinely unpleasant and the odors to which one was treated were original, to say the least.

I was ordered with my men to ordinary garrison duty along the docks and spent my first few months there.

It was following this initial period that I found myself attached to the household of the Roman governor of Judea, one Pontius Pilate. He may be of your acquaintance, and in what follows I intend no unjust criticism of the way in which he handled a difficult and culturally biased situation. One could wish from him, however, a higher and more legitimate grasp of Roman colonial law, and a more open willingness to understand with sensitivity the largely Jewish population and its Hebrew culture with which he must deal daily.

In candor, I must say that Pilate is an interesting mixture of dark and light; thoroughly a politician and an opportunist, caring little for what my Jewish friend of shipboard would have called "righteousness," Pilate yet has some sense of what is appropriate and just in a civil crisis. From months in his palace circle I can also say that he is deeply in love with his wife and is entirely loyal to her. On occasion, she has influenced his actions. In summary, Pilate in his way has tried to exercise his office of Governor to the welfare of all concerned, keeping his eye meanwhile on Rome and his own reputation there.

The Governor spends most of his time in his palace at Caesarea Philippi, well north of the Sea of Galilee and inland from the seaport of Tyre. It is a pleasant place, very Roman for this arid, dry country with its peculiar religious culture. Pilate sees to it that there is no unnecessary talk of gods or of the Hebrew Yahweh in this, his palace retreat.

When I first was ordered to Pilate's company he was in Casearea. It was midwinter and a bit rainy. Time hung heavily on the hands of all of us in the palace guard. There was little to do, certainly nothing to guard. Occasionally, we would be sent out to hunt down a band of Zealots, hyperpatriots who are very resentful of our Roman "yoke," as they call it. These Zealots will fall upon one of our provisioning pack-trains and demolish it, or even now and again they may attack a small squad of soldiers on a lonely road, if they feel they can handle the situation.

We felt strongly that we could brook no insolence from these Jewish people, whatever their social level. There is in all the Hebrew culture a running stream, never far below the surface, of resentment of outsiders, especially ruling outsiders. Our only danger lay in showing any laxity which might have given the signal for an armed civil outbreak.

It was after some months of this comparative inactivity that we heard the news that Pontius Pilate would make his annual trek to Jerusalem for the Passover Feast days. This Passover is possibly the most important annual holiday in the Hebrew calendar, dating back to some obscure occurrence in early Jewish history. The Governor made a point of going down to the capital city on this occasion, in order that his presence would serve as a deterrent to undue public demonstrations or other political activity. His announced purpose, of course, was that he wished to do honor to the Hebrew holy day.

Ordinarily, the Governor occupies the palace of Herod Antipas, the Tetrarch of Galilee, when in the city for this holiday. Herod turns his Jerusalem residence over to the Governor as an act of courtesy which is really somewhat grudging. The two men, in fact, have little liking for each other.

The guards' quarters here are extremely good, considering the usual level of housing in the land. I billeted my men comfortably, divided them into watches for the days ahead, and detailed some of them to street patrol. Following this, I found that as usual I had most of my time on my hands.

It was several days later that I was ordered by Crispus, the Governor's Captain, to take twenty men and hurry to the gate in the main city wall which opens onto the Bethany road to the east. Word had come that a mob was forming out on the Mount of Olives beyond; the report had it that this was a noisy group and that it might be building up around some sort of rabble-rouser or a Zealot hero.

...Your Grace, this, I think, is the point at which the whole history of my tour of duty in Palestine, in fact, the whole direction of my life, began to change. The train of events was started which was to upset completely my thinking, my cherished Roman ideals and my plans for my future.

On this day, with my detail of men I hurried to the Bethany Gate and was just in time to see the beginning of the procession into the city itself. I had intended to disperse it, by force if necessary, and to send the people on their way. But here is what I saw...

First, there was a group of people, mostly women and children, walking in through the gate; they were singing and shouting that the Messiah had come... I was familiar enough with Jewish lore and superstition to know that this Messiah is supposed to be the long-awaited deliverer, the one who will lift the Hebrew nation up before all the nations; he will make the rest of the world merely the footstool of the Hebrews.

This unlikely hope has fierce adherents among young and old, educated and crude alike. It is, in fact, a central key to the great adhesive and united quality of Hebrew culture in the land.

Well — so the Messiah was coming was he? Probably more accurately, the people had picked up some fellow and were using him as an excuse for a procession... I decided to wait a few minutes to see what developed; after all, the people ought to be allowed to express their noisy pleasure and joy so long as it did no harm.

Following the first group of singers there was a second group, waving palm branches and limbs from olive trees in the suburban orchards. Some of these would whip off their outer cloaks and lay them down in the street, obviously for the great man to walk upon. Many of the bystanders on the curb near us were infected with the fever of enthusiasm, and they would step out and join the singers or take off their cloaks and lay them with the others.

I am not sure what I had expected to see, but it certainly was not the small group that was the center of all this excitement... There were perhaps a dozen of them, quiet, rather simple looking men, walking more or less together. It wasn't until they were quite close that I saw that they were surrounding a fellow who was riding a very small colt. His head was hardly above those of the men who were walking near him.

Then a surprising thing happened. As this central group came near our detail of soldiers and they saw us standing in front of the crowds that lined the street, immediately a sort of consternation crossed their faces. Then it was replaced by a kind of dogged determination, as if they were getting ready for a scuffle. I saw them close in tighter around the rider, and then one of them spoke to him and he looked over at us.

Again, I don't know what I expected; I do know that my hand closed over the hilt of my lightsword... Then — the man on the colt caught my eye...

It may be that he smiled: I'm not sure. But the effect of his facial expression was to make me feel as though we knew each other, had perhaps been campaign buddies in some forgotten battle. Then he turned back to the people again, most of whom were ignoring us and cheering as though Rome had set them free. Verily, I believe that this is just what some of them thought was about to happen.

The crowd passed on down the street, not without a nervous backward glance or two on the part of those henchmen of his — and left us standing there feeling a bit foolish.

Quietly, we took our way out into the street to follow, remaining far enough behind so that we wouldn't excite suspicion and start a commotion. When we arrived at the great Temple near the center of the city, we could hear a violent tumult going on inside the walled forecourt; a great crowd stood around outside looking uncertain and confused. We were familiar with the turf-based scuffles that frequently took place among the small merchants inside the courtyard who sold articles to be used in worship in the great building beyond. Here was obviously more of the usual. It was the official policy, however, not to interfere with Hebrew worship customs and never to set foot on temple property.

Thus it was that we turned and wended our way back to our quarters, feeling that this crowd, at least, would give no trouble. My men were quiet on our return walk — unusual for them — and I went to my room and flung myself out on my pallet...

Such a small incident it had been — and yet, in its way, unnerving. *Had* I seen this fellow before? Why his glance my way that had seemed so familiar? But, of course, I knew I hadn't seen him prior to this day... The incident stayed with me somewhere in the back of my mind, but in a few hours, consciously at least, it was forgotten.

I did hear word of the man once or twice as the week wore on; there was even one report that he was healing some who were ill. I laid this simply to popular gossip... My men and I found ourselves occupied with a few minor incidents that occurred as always in the city during Passover week, and I paid little further attention to the memory of the man on the colt.

...It was without warning that on the sixth day of the week my whole sense of inner security, my planned military career, the world as I thought I knew it were all thrown into turmoil.

It began when I was routed at dawn out of deep sleep by a house messenger and told to report at once to the Governor. I dressed hurriedly and entered the palace through the armory door. At once I could hear the low rumble of voices that comes from a large gathering. I strode into the private judgement-room, which was empty, and followed the sound of voices into the main audience chamber. The Governor, it appeared, was on the large outer platform of this room facing the street. I hurried out to him, saluted — and then stared in complete surprise.

You must understand that I wasn't yet fully awake. It came as a jolt, therefore, to recognize on the platform near the Governor the man whom I had seen hailed into the city several days before as the saving Messiah.

His situation was brutally different now. His hands were tied in front of him and his robe bore the marks of rather rough handling. It was clear that a heated controversy was in progress.

I assumed at first that the crowd was protesting because the Governor had seen fit to take their hero captive. As I stood listening, I discovered to my amazement that the situation was precisely the reverse: the Governor was angrily endeavoring to set the man free, while the crowd was demanding that he be punished... I sent a messenger for a few of my legionaries and awaited orders.

The prisoner was standing without a word while the argument waxed furious around him. Once he looked at me, and in embarrassment — I can't explain it, but I *was* embarrassed — I turned my eyes away.

Then the Governor was speaking to me.

"Centurion, this fellow is a Galilean. He should be judged by the Tetrarch of that region. Take him to Herod... I wish not to see him again." Then the Governor turned and disappeared inside.

It was clear immediately that the mob was taken aback. It was a strange group, I noticed, not at all like the joyful throng that had welcomed the man into the city just days before. Here there was a smattering of high temple authorities and quite a few clerks and scribes, but the large bulk of the crowd was riffraff from the slum sections of the city, the very ones who give us the most trouble on high feast days.

I was curious... Why this strange alliance?

All of this went through my mind rapidly while I formed my legionaries into a small guard and motioned to the accused man to follow me. I didn't like the look of the crowd, and I set my men about the prisoner protectively... Meanwhile, the mob had resurrected its angry and accusative spirit and followed us across the city, waking loud early-morning echoes among the still-empty canyons of the streets.

Things did not turn out as expected at the residence to which Herod had betaken himself so that Pilate could occupy his palace. The Tetrarch — many referred to him as "King" Herod — was up and waiting for us, breakfasting with friends. I knew that the hour was unusually early for him, drinker and glutton that he was.

I did him the courtesy of bowing upon being admitted; it went against my grain, but such gestures were required of us as a matter of colonial policy... I explained my mission briefly, and he waved me away.

"I know," he said. "They sent me a messenger. Let me see this surprising fellow."

I almost asked *who* had sent a messenger: I knew that Pilate had no such intention... Then I held my tongue because suddenly I understood, and many things fell into place.

The only ones who could have sent a messenger were the Jewish authorities. This meant that they were determined to see the fellow convicted and punished — all of which explained the early hour and the motley crowd. They were hurrying things through, even though anyone with the slightest knowledge of colonial regulations is aware that to hold trial before the hour of nine in the morning is illegal... And the crowd: of course! Temple authorities scattered among a mob of bought dupes, scum from the slums paid to cry out and make their accusations: false for the most part.

It was then that I discovered an odd thing about myself: both emotionally and rationally, I was on the side of the prisoner. I was actively hoping that he would be released. I told myself that this was because I wanted to see justice done as an officer of Rome. I have come to believe since that there were other motives involved. For one, there was what I can only call *powerful personal affinity* — that strange knowledge when you meet someone for the first time that such a meeting is intended, is perhaps part of a plan, has been waited for... There were still other motivations, soon to make themselves felt.

As I have remarked, things did not go well at Herod's residence. He had heard some of the strange stories about this man's unusual powers; cynically, as though he were dealing with a sorcerer, Herod tried to force him to demonstrate these unique capacities. With a quiet dignity which completed his victory over me, the prisoner repulsed this attempt to make sport of him... Then Herod simply sent us packing back to Pilate, a move which concerned me but over which I had little control.

I began to understand the Governor's desire to be rid of the affair. I don't know how much Pilate had come to know or how much he *felt* concerning this strange prisoner of his, but there was something about the man: extend your sympathy to him even to a small degree, open yourself to the drawing power that was there, and you were lost. You found yourself muttering words to the effect that he was right and you were going to stand by him to the end...

I recognize that I am not saying this well. It is hard not to speak as a Roman, your Grace. In our experience as servants of the Empire, we are owned by it in such a way that the self is submerged; the Empire is larger than the self, all encompassing, with a rule and a demand that is total and impersonal.

In this case, although the feeling was growing on me that this battered, mistreated peasant had won a deep level of my personal allegiance, yet there was no consequent sense of having lost myself. Rather, it was as though I had received something — as though he had given me something of his inward presence and his power in return for what he had been given, or more precisely, what he had taken.

I had meant to give him nothing: he had been nothing to me... But I know now, as surely as I am here in my cell, that he had taken me. He had not said a word to me — but he had taken me.

I realize that much of this may be meaningless to you, your Grace; perhaps I am struggling to explain the inexplicable... It is even possible that he has somehow bewitched me, robbed me of my higher senses. I must say that if this be so, then I am well rid of what I have lost to him: this because life has taken on a certainty, a sense of direction, an inward compulsion that I never knew before he entered my world — on the back of a colt coming through the Bethany Gate.

I can only say, Sir, that I am rich now as I was never rich before. This, too, I find it difficult to define or explain... I believe, though, that knowing me as you do, you will see it in me. If you do not, there is no convincing word I can say to you, because here is precisely the quality this strange prisoner possessed.

He had rich gifts to give, but one had to *see* that richness. If one couldn't, this weary prisoner was nothing: just a peasant from the north country who had gotten himself into trouble. If one *could* see it, he could not help but desire it and find himself in worship before it.

As this awful day wore on, it became all too clear that some folk *could* see it, and many could not.

I have jumped ahead of my planned report, your Grace; all of what I have narrated here, all of this understanding of my own experience of this man, came to me only by degrees, later. But I have given you, I believe, the core message of it.

Events moved swiftly after this... The Governor was not pleased to see us return. I must say in his behalf that Pilate tried several ruses to free the prisoner, becoming increasingly furious as each plan was drowned in the screams of the mob.

Before I was aware of it, the trial was over — and I... I had been assigned the task of seeing to the crucifixion of the prisoner!

My memory of the next few hours is far from clear — perhaps mercifully... I know now that I was far more emotionally and personally involved than at the time I recognized.

As is the brutal custom, the prisoner was made to carry his own cross, a bit of keen cruelty to which I will never become accustomed... We walked slowly because of the prisoner's weary weakness. I suspect that he had slept little and eaten nothing the night before, and I quickly discovered that he had been unnecessarily beaten and systematically mistreated by my own legionaries. In my helpless rage, I determined to confine my men to their quarters later, when I would have opportunity to investigate.

As we walked through the gathering heat of the morning toward a hill outside the Damascus Gate, most of the crowd followed and we picked up curb-watchers as we passed. Just outside the walls of the city, the prisoner fainted. I enlisted a passerby, over his emphatic protest, to carry the cross; he was a big fellow, and strong. I suspect that he, too, began to feel something of this convicted man's strange presence and power, because his grumblings ceased after a few minutes of the walk up the hill; he carried the cross to the top, alone, even when others would have helped him.

It was then, on the way up the hill, that I found myself walking beside the prisoner. Never have I felt less like a Roman officer or cared less about the respect due my station.

At one point the man stumbled and I took his arm... Your Grace, I labor to relate this only very simply, yet I find it difficult... As I took his arm I kept my gaze stiffly to the front, but I felt his eyes on me; he must have read some of the misery I was feeling. We plodded slowly up the hill together and after a bit he spoke to me; it was the only time he did.

"It's all right," he said. "I'm not leaving you."

Strange words... But the strangest thing of all was the way they affected me. They spoke directly to my need, for there had been an unexpected and desolate feeling of loss rolling over me, like an inexorable tide.

At the moment there was no inward asking of questions, no analyzing of my own feelings; all of this came later. I recall at this point only a curious and vast relief... This man knew. He accepted my unspoken fealty, my strange loyalty, my sense of need — even as I must proceed to take his life. He knew and accepted.

The crucifixion followed the usual brutal pattern, except that the man's reactions all the way through, even in intense pain, were as unexpected as they had been all morning. After we raised the cross, he hung there almost in silence, uttering not a word for minutes at a time; it was as though he were trying to ease the unpleasantness of the thing for those who were watching. The effect of all of this on the gaping crowd was not surprising: after a few of the usual taunts, silence fell; soon, by ones and twos, they began to leave — highly unusual given the situation and the character of the mob.

The morning sun was beating down now with a merciless fury, unusual in late springtime in this place. I sat a little apart, facing the vast valley below us; I couldn't abide the gaping faces of the crowd, though, as I've said, the people had grown silent now with a common spirit of wonder: this man was leading us all through the experience of death with him... There is no other way I can describe what was happening.

He had broken through to some of them: I know it now. There were a few who felt the loss — and the gain — of it.

There were two or three, in fact, who sought me out — deeply puzzled at the reaction they were feeling.

"Who — what —" one began to ask.

I answered without conscious intent.

"This man...was a son of God."

I have no recollection of how long I sat there, as near to mental oblivion as I have ever been in my life. When I finally came to myself I looked up at the cross. The man was dead.

Somehow, I hadn't expected it.

For a few moments I was overwhelmed. Then my sudden feeling of intense personal loss was just as suddenly replaced by an exhilarating knowledge... I have thought long on how to put it into words that will carry the simple truth: *it was as though he had taken me by the arm and had shown me that death is a lie.*

I believe, your Grace, that the rest of my story is well known to you. I left the hilltop and returned to the palace, pausing there only long enough to have a mount saddled in the stables. I rode straight to Joppa; there was a ship being made ready and I took passage.

Once again, I am grateful for being permitted to tell my story. I am quite aware, your Grace, as I said at the beginning of this long account — aware of Rome's dealings with a deserting officer.

I have desired to live, as I have been gazing from my prison window, and yet it may be that I have lived long enough. There will be very few of the others who will be privileged to tell their story before a high tribunal of Rome...for there will be others, I know — others there on the hilltop who felt what he was, this strange man on his cross.

You will hear further of him, your Grace. You will hear further because the others will not be able to hide it, to keep it in. It cannot be kept within — once one has been taken by it... Just as he said to me, it is all right, for he has not left us: he is loose upon the world.

Strangely, his name I never knew... But *you* will know, when you hear of him again.

When you do, recall my words. He showed it beyond question to me and to others: *death is a lie.*

He has mastered it — and none of us who accept life inspired and given new form by him...need fear death ever again.

Chapter 6

Barabbas

Time is cruel — the passing of time, that is. There is no way to resurrect what of time has been allowed to pass in tragedy, to take it in hand again and fashion it anew. Time is unforgiving, and it rewards or punishes with unfeeling precision.

Of all men who have ever lived, I was the most prepared to welcome my death. I had chosen each step of the way — the way downward as I see it now — and after my many dragging days in the city's lowest dungeon, even the cross which I heard them preparing in the yard above was promise of relief.

Here was the logical climax of the statement I had sought my life to make; for a long period — actually many months — I had been aware that for me and mine there could be only one conclusion. The sole question remaining was the matter of how and when the dramatic ending would come upon me.

Then the unaccountable occurred. Another man went to the cross which they had intended for me: life suddenly stretched on before me, dressed in unfamiliar and shocking colors.

I wasn't ready for life because I had so readied myself for death...

Surely you must be aware that this is not the way my story ends... Time has slowly reversed its cruelty; I have come to value and to give thanks for each succeeding hour I am granted — each hour he gave me when he climbed the hill that day to accept *my* cross.

My childhood years were rich with thoughtlessly accepted privilege. I was born into a very religious family — religious in the best sense known to our ancient Hebrew tradition.

It will strike you as sharp irony that at birth I was called "Jesus" — simply the somewhat Hellenized form of our Hebrew "Joshua." It is a name much beloved among us, with its linguistic rootage in the claim "Yahweh saves" — the Lord redeems. This, of course, was the holy promise that bound our people together in hope — even as we bore the apparently hopeless yoke of subjugation to Rome.

My father was something of a lawyer in his earlier days, having specialized in the study of the heritage and customs under which Jewish national life was carried on. It was always an easy step, however, from this over into the teaching priesthood, as it was commonly recognized. Before I was ten years old, my father became a respected Teacher of the Law. It was in this capacity that he dedicated his full time to the teaching of young men in the synagogue schools about the ancient story of Israel. Central to this was his concern to instill precise knowledge of the development of the Torah, our sacred Book of Law.

It was after my father assumed this authoritative position that I began increasingly to be called simply "the Teacher's son" — or Bar-abbas.

It was inevitable that as I child I should have been taught a deep reverence for the things of the spirit, and as deep a reverence for the holy history of our people. We were bound closely in prayer as a family, for it was the custom for orthodox families to pray at certain stated times of the day, without fail. This was one of the central burdens of our religious and cultural heritage.

In view of all of this, it was not strange that I early developed an intense pride in my Hebrew lineage. It was literally drummed into me, morning, noon and night, that ours was the chosen people of Yahweh; as such, we bore responsibility to bring our faith and practice to the heathen wherever and however we should find him.

Our God had signally honored us, and, more than any other people of earth, we were called not only to be the messengers of his method among all mankind, but also we were destined to be lifted to a zenith among the nations. The day would come when we, the Hebrew people, would have the world as our footstool. All the peoples of earth would come up in reverence and praise to our Holy Hill.

It follows that I was given every advantage of education and culture. The importance of my father's position in our city increased with each passing year. I attended the synagogue schools and did well, this success coming quite naturally to me: I had been raised from tenderest years in the very atmosphere of the subjects under study.

The change was unexpected and unplanned in its coming... It began in quick drama and peril, but continued as a gradual mutation...

There is danger attached to belonging to a religious and cultured heritage. The danger is that one rarely appreciates the blessing of it until a passing of the years has put it into true and accurate focus. More — it brings with it its strictures: the honoring of God in family life does not conjoin certain other social pressures. Either worship and principle are sacrificed, or some attractive personal pleasures are to be avoided: one cannot enjoy both and he makes his choice.

It was in later youth that I made mine, and it proved fateful beyond severest expectation.

I encountered the fellow on the Street of Shops one hot noon. He was lounging in the shade, as was I. About my own age, he arrested my attention by the concentration with which he watched the approach of a lone Roman officer; this worthy was swaggering more than half drunk up the street, pushing people out of his way and cursing loudly.

I realized then that the young man in the shade only appeared to be lounging; actually, his body was tense and ready. I was spellbound; I didn't realize how close I was to him until after it had happened.

As the Roman came abreast of us, the young man quickly and quietly stepped through the crowd; I followed. There was a glint of sunlight on metal as his dagger flashed. With a hideous scream the Roman fell to the earth at my feet.

Instinctively I knew the officer would die and that I had been too close to the affair for safety. I broke through the ring of people that had instantly formed and took to my heels — after the retreating figure of the young Jew. I followed him through several streets and alleys as he beat a zigzag route; I was hardly aware of what I was doing.

I had heard of the out-of-sight sect called Zealots, but I had never encountered one of them — or if I had, I wasn't aware of it. Most people weren't aware of them even when talking to one. The

Zealots... Fired by an intense love of nation and heritage, they held fast to their conviction that the day of triumph for Israel was not far distant.

I had never understood the basis of their assumption that Yahweh was about to bring in the new day. Surely the people of our Palestine had never suffered such subjection, carefully smoothed over with Roman justice, as they experienced under their current overlords. However, these Zealots, hot-blooded and burning to free their people and fight for the triumph of Israel, would stop at nothing to fall upon a thinly defended Roman pack-train in the desert, or to pick off occasional lone messengers on horseback in the mountains, or — as in this instance, to wipe out a Roman soldier with his defenses temporarily down.

As a youngster, I had asked my father about the Zealots. All boys love tales of adventure, and tend to make heroes out of those who create adventure. My father had spoken in no uncertain terms.

"These Zealots," he said, "are misunderstanding the whole teaching of our Scriptures. Israel will simply never be a great warlike nation; look at its size and power as compared to Rome or Athens. True, our God will bring in the golden destiny of Israel one day, but it will be through his own means — not the sharpened knives of these foolish brigands of ours."

On another occasion, my father had remarked, "God does not work his will with swords. He works with men's minds and men's hearts."

On this my first encounter with the Zealots, this headlong race through the streets, the young man whose running feet I had been following suddenly stopped and he turned on me.

Almost fiercely he said, "Why are you following me?"

I mumbled that I hadn't really meant to follow him, that I had been afraid — afraid that they would accuse me of the lawless murder.

"Lawless!" he scoffed. "There is no law but the law of Judah." His eyes were hostile.

When he asked, "Who are you?" I told him.

"Poof!" he said. "You sons of the wealthy!"

My temper was stirring. My breathing was easier now after the rapid running, and I offered to take him on in a wrestling match — without daggers, of course.

His attitude changed. He looked at me, at first curiously and than calculatingly. Then, "Come with me!" he said, and turned on his heel.

Thus it happened that I met the Zealots. I was seventeen at the time, and in search of a goal in life that would attract and hold me. As I have indicated, life during my growing years within our family had been rich and full, but — and here the danger I have alluded to earlier evidenced itself — like many privileged and protected youngsters, I craved adventure. The Zealots offered it, together with a shallow and immature nationalism that I thought at the time very noble.

At first, I merely accompanied some of them on an occasional foray, "to observe," as I told myself repeatedly. The inevitable occurred: when one puts oneself in contact with any steady influence, whether it be destructive or supportive, he begins to think it, to breathe it, to become it.

I told my family nothing. I realized later that they had known all along, and suffered in silence. In less than a year I was forced to leave Jerusalem, not by my parents but because suddenly and to my surprise, I realized that I had become a hunted man. The Romans made short work of a Zealot when he was caught; there would be a brief trial, lasting perhaps ten minutes. If there were any Roman ties, there would be a beheading. For most of us, native to Palestine and citizens only of our own land, our hands were tied to the patibulum, the horizontal beam of a cross, and we were taken out to slow and agonizing death.

It was inevitable that I would find increasing fascination in the life I was leading, pillaging and harassing the Romans at any opportunity. To my youthful and shallow insight, the prospect of a cross seemed remote: such things happened only to older and more dull people. At nineteen, I killed my first man, and thereafter it became increasingly easy to kill.

I was living now in the desolate hills north of the Jericho road with a band of ten others. I recall one twilight moment of rest; I was sitting on a broad rock watching the sunset far to the west. In a moment of rare introspection, I asked myself how it had happened to me, how I had become one of them, too wise and too practiced and too hardened now to stop. The blood of twenty-three men was on my hands.

I thought back over my childhood, to a world that seemed in another age now. How had it happened, this strange, swift change of character, of the priorities, of life?

As I pondered, I realized that it had been absurdly easy: take one false step, depart momentarily from one's ingrained values, to observe only — and one was on his way. A fleeting lack of self-control, a brief voluntary forgetting of certain basic truths: it hadn't been difficult, I thought ruefully.

The inevitable day came when Ishmael, our leader, was caught with a bloody dagger in his tunic as he was coming out of the East Gate of the city. I became the acknowledged head of our band. I had just turned twenty-one and I was troubled and a bit frightened by new responsibility. I had not seen my parents for three years, and they were hardly four miles away in the city...

One hot spring morning I was walking by myself in a lonely canyon, whiling away the dangerous daylight hours. I rounded a large boulder and came upon a man sitting in the shade of it. My hand leapt to the concealed handle of my dagger, and then came away. He was just a peasant...

I passed without a word and continued on my way, feeling his eyes upon my back. I had taken not a dozen steps when I heard his voice, low and quite companionable.

"Friend, have you lost your way?"

It was a strange question, strangely fitting. I turned and looked at him. He was sitting just where I had passed him, relaxed, rather weary looking.

I started to speak, and then the wariness of the hunted took possession of me. I turned and continued on my way. He didn't speak again. At the top of the ridge, I looked back; he was still sitting there, still watching me.

I hurried on, with that casual-sounding question haunting me. "Friend, have you lost your way?"

I slept little that night, and I cursed the strange peasant wordlessly. He had known that I was not lost in the hills. He had meant something else. What was it?

In honest reflection, I suspected that he had sensed the strange split within me. At the very least I knew my need: he had spoken so accurately to it — either intentionally or by pure chance.

Ideals... The high ideals by which I had pledged myself to the cause of ridding my native land of its conqueror. The strength of my youth and my weapon: these I had put at the service of my country...

Or — had I? Had the ideal somewhere along the way been lost in the method? Was I now killing for the very love and excitement of it? Had a new motivation entered in, to displace the high dreams of my earlier religious patriotism?

How easily it had happened... I had offered myself recklessly to the service of my country and my God — and then, somewhere and somehow along the way, I had forgotten both.

The lust... The dulling effect of constant force and brutality... The shining armor — that was shining only until you began to use it. The weapons of force, of which at first you were the master, but which so soon mastered you: had all of these subtly and ruthlessly taken over?

Thus it was that I tossed upon my pallet and stared sleeplessly at the stars overhead.

Had I for so long now been travelling down the wrong road? Didn't you really win your point by having a sharper sword than the other fellow? After all, I had offered Yahweh my strength and my agility with weapons. These were practical gifts, useful, and he should have honored them by giving me clarity of purpose and vision. Blessed by the Almighty, doesn't a man have to make his dreams come true by carving them out with his own hands?

Then, as dawn was lightening the eastern sky, I knew the truth, knew it for what it was and indelibly... Jacob had once wrestled all night, and now so had I. The truth...

All the while the clear reality had been there, but I had struggled to sidestep it: no man can serve two masters, not when they are at odds with one another.

The Almighty plants the dream, the ideal. Then there are two ways open to one, and he makes his choice. There is the quick and self-serving way of force, the dashing, colorful way which demands that one forget the niceties and cut more and more of the corners. Or — there is the slow and painful way of creating an alternative — building toward the truth.

The first way, by its very character, blunts the dream. A man one day lives for force alone: the ideal has subtly vanished... The second way is difficult because it is slow and costly in terms of display and self-satisfaction — but the dream stays, hard and clear and shining.

"Friend, have you lost your way?"

Quietly, in the cool of the dawn, I stole from our hideaway and walked with firm steps toward the city. Danger was ever-present there, but there were a few more things I had to know before I would be sure what to do. This peasant had been a stranger, and therefore he would be lodging temporarily in the city. I needed to find him; then, perhaps...

At the Damascus Gate, the early morning camel trains leaving for the sea coast blocked my way; I became impatient and consequently careless. I pushed through them, attracting the loud curses of the camel-drivers and the attention of a Roman garrison squad.

Two minutes later, I felt a heavy hand on my shoulder. I turned to confront a sergeant who was swiftly searching me in quest of a hidden weapon. I broke from his grip and ran straight into the arms of two other guards. Resistance was useless...

Within the hour I found myself in one of the lower and damper dungeons in the ancient city prison. The only light came from a tiny hole high up in the wall and a crack or two in the upper brickwork. It was hard to keep track of day and night.

Toward the end of my weeks of sojourn in this hellish place, I heard the hammers and saws of the carpenters. I knew what was under construction: I had been living too long in the shadow of the executioner to have any illusions.

I had been longing for many things as these lonely days dragged by — a word with my parents, the sight of a familiar face; it would not have taken much to cheer my heart. Too, I missed more elemental things — a look at light, at the sun, the smell of fresh air.

The prospect of death no longer frightened me; it even became welcome as time wore on...and my thoughts: what a transformation I underwent in the silence and blackness. The strange peasant had given me far more than he would ever know.

"Friend, have you lost your way?"

I heard the tramp of the soldiers' feet descending the stair, heard it without fear. The heavy door opened, and I was being led upward — helped upward. I had been so weakened that climbing was impossible without a helping arm.

So suddenly that I caught my breath, I was thrust forth into the glaring sunlight of early morning; I stumbled onto a large stone platform beyond which was a yelling, jostling throng. On the platform there were two or three palace underlings, a soldier or two, the Governor himself, and, of all people — my strange peasant of the little valley.

It was with difficulty that I recognized him. He was dressed in a smeared and stained tunic, his hands bound and his forehead bloody from some twisted thorn-branches that had apparently been forced down upon it; vestiges of the cruel crown were still there. He looked at me and a smile formed: he remembered the valley...

Then things happened so rapidly that in my weakened state I could only partly grasp them at the time. I recall that the Governor raised his hand for silence and spoke to the crowd. There was a brief pause while a messenger presented a letter to the Governor. For a few moments he glanced at it; he looked over at the other prisoner. I think he was about to speak, when someone shouted my name and then another joined in. Suddenly the cry of "Barabbas!" was coming from every quarter of the crowd.

With sudden shock, I knew what was happening. This glaring morning, already hot, was the beginning of the Passover; how could I have forgotten? The Governor was allowing the crowd to choose what single prisoner would be released; it was an act of clemency practiced by Rome as a small concession to our holy day.

This stranger — no, this brief acquaintance of mine from the hills — this man was being offered to the crowd along with myself. My weakened legs suddenly felt as though they would collapse and I struggled for balance.

The shouting lessened momentarily, and I heard the Governor calling my name. I was pushed roughly off the platform and down into the crowd. A great new shout went up, and for a moment I thought the mob was about to carry me on its shoulders.

As suddenly as my name had been called from every quarter, I was forgotten, and then I knew: the crowd had not been intent on saving me; it had merely been intent on convicting my peasant acquaintance.

My mind was still slow, as if I had been drugged. I had been almost without food for several days toward the end of my imprisonment and I had been alone for an eternity in the dark and damp of the dungeon. The rapid sequence of activity was almost too much for me.

I turned and looked toward the platform. Pilate, the Governor, was drying his hands after dipping them into a bowl. A squad of soldiers was leading the other fellow away; they moved off the platform and over to where the loosely-tied beams of a cross lay on the cobbled square.

A shock of sudden recognition brought me fully to my senses: this man was going to the cross in my place. A miracle had occurred! I was free — free! I was free to hunt up my parents, free to take up a new sort of life.

A new sort of life... Why — this was the fellow who had given me that new sort of life, just by the few words he had spoken to me out there in the hills. First, he had saved me inwardly — yes, spiritually. That came clear now, as my numbness wore off. First that inward act, and now he had saved me physically: they would put him on the cross they had prepared for me...

I had to know more. I turned to a rough man of the streets walking beside me. Most of us had joined the procession, larger than was usual in such cases, following the prisoner as he half dragged and half carried his cross toward the execution hill outside of town.

"What has this fellow done?" I asked. "Who is he?"

My companion grunted. "Don't know who he is, but I was paid pretty well to join the crowd and shout against him." Then, defensively, "A fellow has to eat! I was hungry."

Almost breathless, I asked again, "But what did he do?"

"I dunno. Ask somebody else."

I asked several others, without much satisfaction. Putting the pieces of what I heard together, it seemed that the man had been some sort of a public trouble-maker; it also appeared that the temple authorities had paid a number of people and brow-beaten others into joining the rabble. The assignment seemed to coalesce around influencing the Governor by sheer volume of noise to have the man executed.

I hadn't heard of this sort of thing ever before. My father had always held the temple authorities up as the moral leaders of our people. Why had they done this?

The procession wound its way noisily out of the city and up the Hill of the Skull, as it is called. The crowd seemed almost in a picnic mood; it was a holiday, and here was something interesting to break the monotony of the hours ahead.

Then I was at the top of the hill, and my hunger and weakness were forgotten. It suddenly became crucial that I see this fellow face to face, to speak to him, to tell him what he had done for me, to hear his voice again. Strange as it may seem, I knew in that moment that something was very wrong. This man was going to my cross, and I felt almost as though I should not have allowed it. *I* should have gone...

I pushed my way through the crowd. It was hard to do, and took a long time; everybody wanted to see at first hand. Finally I broke into the inner circle — and I was too late. They had brutally nailed the victim's hands and feet to the cross and already they were lifting it into the air to drop it into its socket in the ground. The man's eyes were closed — whether in pain or prayer I couldn't tell.

Moments later, his voice *was* quietly audible in prayer; those of us standing near could discern what he was saying. The crowd, in the presence of suffering and to its own surprise, had been moved to silence. I caught his words, seared across my memory as if with a blacksmith's hot iron.

"Father," the man was praying, "forgive them, for they know not what they do..."

I have no recollection of how long I stood there near the cross. I don't know what I hoped for: that the man would notice me there below him, perhaps, and let me speak to him...or touch him.

I waited in vain. Only once did he seem to notice the crowd, and this was when he spoke briefly out of his agony to a young man standing beside a woman who was weeping broken-heartedly. The hot hours wore on. Slowly the crowd had dispersed in twos and threes back to the city.

Still, there I stood... My cross, but I wasn't hanging from it. That should have been I suffering there: instead, this man.

There was no coherence in the several reports of his crime that I had been given during the walk up the hill. One thing, however, had come though with undeniable clarity: either the priests and authorities my father had so honored had been sadly misled — or they were a pack of scoundrels far worse than I.

Then the priests were forgotten.

As I gazed at this dying figure of a man, I knew that I was faced with a profound debt, coupled with a task. Nothing I might have said or done could have saved him. But — whoever he was, he had changed my life with a word, and then he had died in my stead... Perhaps as he had partaken of my death, I could take up his life. Perhaps...

Certainly he must have had friends. Beginning in the city, but moving across the world if need be, I would find them. Surely what he had done for me with a word, he must have done for others, countless others. My life, such as it was, a poor thing, degraded and weak — my life was his, completely. He had earned it, earned everything I now was and yet could be. In those moments, it broke upon me that nothing else in the world and beyond would really matter...

The distillation of all of this, this experience of a man going to his death in my place literally, physically, on a particular day that I could always name and the memory of which I encounter continually, even hourly — the meaning of it all came into focus only slowly. As I had early suspected, the man had friends, followers, even committed disciples. I sought them out, found answers to the questions that were torturing me, and discovered that there was a program overarching their future to which a growing number of these were dedicated everlastingly.

For some of them, no questions remained. Gradually, bathed in the light of their faith and — yes — their ecstasy, I became one with their total commitment.

This was never a choice I made. For me, of choice there was none. This man had taken to himself the death that was to have been mine. Then, moving beyond this, he had acted to give my life perspective, meaning, direction, power, openness, trust: all of these, and I knew that his death had only opened the door for him somehow to become personally operative in my life — the life that I had picked up when he had laid it aside.

None of this was clear to me at the outset, and not for months thereafter. Among those who had known him in life, however, were some who understood the singularity of my situation, the depth of my indebtedness; with care and concern they helped me learn

One moment in time — in memory — I could never lay aside. The scene had been laid in a little valley in the northern hills, when he had watched me walk by and had followed my retreating steps with a question.

"Friend, have you lost your way?"

The End